THE BIG Reveal

The Big Reveal
By Eve Francis

Published by Less Than Three Press LLC

All rights reserved. No part of this book may be used or reproduced in any manner without written permission of the publisher, except for the purpose of reviews.

Edited by Emilia Vane
Cover designed by Natasha Snow

This book is a work of fiction and all names, characters, places, and incidents are fictional or used fictitiously. Any resemblance to actual people, places, or events is coincidental.

First Edition June 2016
Copyright © 2016 by Even Francis
Printed in the United States of America

Digital ISBN 9781620048108
Print ISBN 9781620048467

Jessica & Travis

EVE FRANCIS

Chapter One

Samus was early. When she arrived at the environment building on campus and headed to the fourth floor classroom, it was empty. After uttering a small "oh" under her breath, she pulled out her phone to check the time.

1:50. A smile spread across her lips. No way was she over half an hour early. And on her first day of the semester? *Man, maybe things are going to go right this time around.*

Samus stepped inside the classroom and closed the door behind her. One side of the room was made of glass, which looked directly out on the stairwell, so Samus could still peek out and see the second half of the environment wing and any approaching students from her desk. She had no idea why her English classes always got slotted in the most random rooms (last year, it was in the psychology wing, and the year before that, it was close to the library, which actually made some sense), but she figured it had more to do with her students than her professional standing in the department. She normally taught, alongside a bunch of other first and second year PhDs, the standard "Introduction to English" course that was mostly about how to write a proper essay and a required course for most of the science majors.

Which was a fine course, really. How to write an essay could sometimes be a challenge to teach, since not everyone had the same high school education, and Samus got to know her students well and play to their strengths. But most of the time, the intro classes were super easy and a bore; she often put it as her last priority, which frequently made her late to her own classes.

But not today.

This semester, she would be teaching her course by herself. No reporting to an ornery professor higher up. No attending a boring lecture at nine AM so she could then repeat everything in a class later on that week. And no more grading first year papers. This time, Samus was the instructor of a Fantasy Literature class. She designed the syllabus, the assignments, and picked the book list. The full course name was something like "Imagining the Future & Negotiating the Past: Advanced Studies in Fantasy, Sci-fi, and Speculative Fiction." What that basically meant for Samus was a lot of talk about spaceships, swords and sorcery, and maybe even playing a D&D game in class.

That actually gives me an idea... Since she was early, Samus pulled out her syllabus for review. She had finalized it way back in September when she was first offered the contract, and hadn't put down anything to do with game fantasy landscapes. She couldn't believe the course had gone this far without at least putting in a nod to gaming of some kind, especially since that was Samus's own research area for her PhD. She penciled in D&D on the fifth class session, which was about dragons, before she heard a knock at the door.

"Yes?" Samus said.

A tall woman stood in the doorway to the classroom. She shuffled her feet, eyeing the empty desks in front.

"Are you looking for the Fantasy class?" Samus asked.

"Oh? Oh. No. I'm... Crap. I thought this room was empty. I mean—I saw you in the window, but this class is usually empty around this time, at least last semester it was. Um..." The woman touched her messenger bag strap that was covered in patches. Samus thought she recognized some of them, but wasn't sure.

"No worries. Are you looking for a study space?"

The woman nodded.

"You can stay if you want. I'll have a class in here at 2:30, but feel free to hang around until then."

"Really? That would be great. Thank you. I won't be long. Just waiting for the bus, really."

"Sure, go ahead." Samus smiled and gestured to a desk. The woman stepped forward and took a seat at the farthest one in the corner, close to the door. Once the woman had taken off her messenger bag, Samus noted the design on her T-shirt underneath her open grey hoodie. *Was that Dorian Pavus from* Dragon Age*?*

"You sure you're not in my fantasy lit class?"

The woman smiled. She had one binder open

in front of her, but wasn't too enthralled by the writing. "Nah. But I wish! I had no idea the school even offered a course like that."

"Oh, yeah. Usually for upper year English students."

"Ah, there's the issue. I'm in fourth year for math."

"But you've taken an English class before, right?" Samus said. She knew the answer would be yes before the woman said it aloud. She would have had to take an English course in order to graduate in math. *Was that why she was so familiar?* Samus wondered. *Have I taught her before? Or is it just the random* Dragon Age *connection?*

"I have," the woman confirmed. "But English was never my strongest suit. I stick to math now."

"But still. If you've taken that one English class, then you're eligible for mine. I think the class is full to capacity right now, but you never know what will happen in the next two weeks. I could get a mass exodus after they read the syllabus." Samus laughed. Really, this was her worst fear. Even when her class had capped at twenty-five in a matter of hours of open registration, she had been so afraid this was all a trick. The students would come to her class, sit down and see her, and run away terrified. The worst part about that fate was that in the environmental building, with glass walls everywhere, Samus would have to watch them go. Or worse, Samus would watch them turn around as soon as they took one look at their queer, trans course leader.

"I doubt that. But what's on your syllabus?"

"Oh. Lots of things. I'm actually thinking of adding some D&D to the Dragons week. But here." Samus got up from her desk at the front of the room and wandered over to where the other woman sat. She gave her a spare syllabus and kept one for herself. "I'm Samus, by the way. Samus Mallory."

"Professor Mallory?" the woman asked.

"No, just call me Samus. Or Sam. Both work."

"Good to know. I'm Jacqueline, but everyone calls me Jackie." She extended her hand and Samus shook it right away.

"Nice to meet you."

"I... I actually think I've met you before," Jackie confessed. Her eyes were on the syllabus, her words almost a whisper. "I'm pretty sure you taught my introduction to English class years and years ago."

"Oh?" Samus froze for a moment, praying that she had never had a face-to-face class with Jackie. "When would that be?"

"Um. 2011? No, later than that. Maybe 2013? I can't remember; my time at Waterloo all blends together. But it was an online course."

Samus let out a relieved sigh. "Oh. That was when I first started my PhD here. So yes, 2013 is right, and in that case, you were probably one of my first online students."

"Really?" Jackie smiled again. "Neat. It was certainly over my head. English is already hard enough, but I thought it'd be so much easier online. So wrong."

"Same here, actually. I thought teaching it would be much easier. Turns out, I almost got carpel tunnel from so much grading." Samus held her wrist to emphasize her point. Jackie made a few noises of sympathy before looking back to the syllabus in front of her. She seemed to be completely in awe with the texts chosen, squealing over the fact that Samus had put the recent issue of *Ms. Marvel* on.

"Comic books? You're really allowed to study that in university?"

"Oh, yeah! Of course. The higher you get in English, the more you can get away with. I'm actually doing my dissertation on video games."

"No way! That's amazing. Maybe I should have stuck with it. Especially if I didn't have to do an online course. A bit late now, though. Since I graduate in a few months."

"Never too late," Samus insisted. "Bram Stoker didn't start writing until he was in his forties and his first novel flopped. If he hadn't kept going, we would never have gotten *Dracula*. So there's always time to go back and do what you want, especially if you suddenly find something new to capture your attention."

Jackie shrugged. She tried to push the conversation onto *The Left Hand of Darkness*, since Le Guin's *Earthsea Trilogy* was on the syllabus; Samus went willingly into the conversation, asking Jackie about her favourite Le Guin book, then about the awful adaptation of the *Earthsea Trilogy*. Samus wasn't usually this cheery and open. She hated being disturbed, especially when it was her first day back after a short winter vacation. *But this class already has me beyond excited. For the first time in a long, long time.* And this new girl was another added bonus.

Even while sitting, Jackie was tall; standing she would probably be at least a few inches above Samus's almost five-ten frame—maybe even as much as six feet. Jackie hunched a lot, as if trying to undermine her own height. Her wrists, when they peaked out of her grey hoodie, were thin and delicate. The rest of her, outside of her baggy clothing, was probably just as thin, too. Her hair was dark and straight, falling against her tanned cheeks and skin.

Jackie also really knew fantasy, and as some of Samus's actual registered students began to show up, Samus realized just how much she wanted Jackie to stay.

"I think I should go now," Jackie said when the fourth student came in. She closed her binder, sighing a bit. "I've gotta get the bus before the snow storm hits us anyway."

"Oh. Okay. Do me a favour, though? Keep the syllabus."

"Really?"

"Oh yeah. Just in case a spot opens up. And if one doesn't, maybe you can study this stuff on your own time."

Jackie laughed a bit at the suggestion.

Did you really just tell a girl you find cute to go and study more? Ridiculous. But Samus recovered quickly. "Or maybe you can come in during the D&D day. You seem to know what you're talking about there, so we may need more experienced DMs."

"Hmm. Maybe. Thank you." Jackie tucked the syllabus into her binder then swung her messenger bag over her chest. "Good luck with your class."

"Thanks. Good luck with your bus." The words felt weird and stilted from Samus's mouth, but she didn't care. She really hoped the students in her classroom didn't see that she was totally flirting, but if they did, so what? *If they realize you're trans, they may as well realize you're also really gay, too.*

After Jackie waved, Samus went back to her desk. More students came inside and took their seats and Samus went over the syllabus again, readjusting the D&D day for the week just after they talked about Dragons. By the time she was done her new reconfiguring, it was already 2:32pm.

Ah well. Late again. But so, so worth it.

Chapter Two

By the time Samus finished her class, it was snowing. As she walked down the environmental building's staircase, all the windows outside seemed to be covered in a thin layer of white. Sighing, Samus pulled out the scarf she had knit and wrapped it around herself. Her short hair made it so her neck was always impossibly cold, so she thanked her lucky stars for remembering to bring her giant green scarf for today.

She trudged through the snow across campus until she came to the Grad House—a coffee bar and pub for all graduate students at Waterloo University.

As soon as she stepped inside, she was accosted by Lindsey. "You! You look like you've been making snow angels."

"No, just walking from the Environmental Sec."

Lindsey let out a low whistle. She tugged off her apron as she stepped into the dining area from the kitchen and glanced out a window. "Shit. Is the storm already that bad?"

"Apparently. Never have I been happier for not owning a car. Winter driving is the worst."

"Instead we have to contend with angry bus drivers. Crap." Lindsey ran a hand through her dark hair then glanced back at the kitchen. The

Grad House's chef stood and watched the two of them with narrowed eyes. "Do you mind if I finish up? Then I'll meet you at our booth?"

"So long as you bring the usual, I'm set."

"Excellent." Lindsey knocked the swinging door with her hip to get back inside the kitchen, saluting Samus as she did. "I will see you in a few minutes, bounty hunter."

Samus laughed before heading upstairs.

~~*

Over a plate of fries and a giant pitcher of Diet Coke, Samus and Lindsey caught up. Lindsey, another PhD student in the English department, had been slotted with teaching the intro to English all over again. Though it was only Wednesday, and the third day into the winter semester, Lindsey was already fuming.

"It's the Goddamn online version of this course," she complained, cramming some fries into her mouth. "And while I don't mind that, I have to deal with Bethany Wright."

"Bethany Wright?" Samus repeated. "The pedagogy prof?"

"Exactly! She's our supervisor, but she insists on pulling us in for meetings once a week to talk about the course. I mean, what's there to talk about? We grade stuff kids hand in. We're making machines. But *no*, Bethany Wright wants to talk about our *feelings* about the course and how much we enjoy teaching. *What's your teaching philosophy?*" Lindsey imitated a pedantic voice then rolled her eyes. "It's like group therapy, only she's the one traumatizing us."

"Really? Wow. I'm even happier I don't have that class."

"I know. You're sitting pretty right now. I mean, I know it's like ten times more work to do your own class, rather than being shunted along for this carnival ride, but at least you have control over your destiny, you know? I feel as if I'm lost to the wolves."

"Bethany's not really a wolf though. More like..."

"A really annoying ankle dog? That barks at wind?"

"I was going to say elf or something else related to fantasy, but hey, I'll go with you."

Lindsey scrunched up her nose, laughing again before she took a long drink of Diet Coke. Samus and Lindsey met during the first orientation week at Waterloo. Though Samus had done her Masters in the same department, this had been when she still thought she was a guy. A really awkward and bitter guy, but still legally a guy on all forms. Applying to Waterloo again for her PhD, when she was twenty-five and still working out whether or not she wanted to be called Samus or Samantha, was a completely unreal experience. Samus had been sure that as soon as she showed up for PhD orientation, everyone would know who she was and who she had been. But instead, during a really awkward social at a local pub, it had been Lindsey who walked up to her with a completely determined stare on her face, and declared,

"Samus... Samus... I know that name. Where is it from?" As soon as Samus said the words "Metroid" and "space bounty hunter," Lindsey clung to her arm and talked video games all night.

The two had been virtually inseparable ever since. Though Lindsey's area of research was in Virginia Woolf and feminist rhetoric during modernism, they often brainstormed and studied together.

Samus finished her section of fries before she poured the rest of the Diet Coke from the pitcher into her glass. Lindsey nodded it was okay for Samus to finish it off.

"So, how was your fantasy class?" Lindsey asked. "I feel bad complaining about my own ordeal, especially when grading online still allows me to keep the job at Grad House since it's less face-time on campus."

"It was... okay. I guess." Samus sipped her drink, her eyes averted.

"Just okay?" Lindsey asked skeptically. "I thought this was the be-all, end-all of classes. Your favourite syllabus, where you could say everything you wanted to say during the lectures."

"No, my dissertation is where I can rant like that. But... I don't know. The class was fine, I guess."

"Oh no. What happened?"

"Nothing, really. I gave out the syllabus, answered questions, and did a brief lesson on the history of sci-fi, using Mary Shelley as one of the first texts."

"Okay. Nice. And?"

"And..." Samus trailed off. How could she really articulate this sudden disappointment? She was under no illusions of how her teaching would go. So many first year PhDs wanted each class to become *Dead Poets Society* and inspire change in the eyes of her students. But that was rarely the case. If you could shift that focus from inspiring to just having fun, then it was often better. And really, Samus thought the class had had fun today.

"I did an ice breaker and they talked about their favourite movies. But that was about it. I don't know. It'll be better next time, I'm sure."

"Of course. First classes are always hard. You'll get the hang of it. " Lindsey said, taking out her notebook from her bag. "So I can stop talking in clichés, will you be so kind as to humour me for our weekend plans?"

"Right." Samus put down her drink and pulled out her phone. This had been the real reason to meet after class—in addition to catching up with one another. They both had a conference together in London, Ontario, at Western University, a couple hours away, and needed to hammer out the finer details.

"I booked us the room in a close-by hotel," Lindsey stated. "I confirmed your registration when I did mine as well. So that only leaves us with a car."

"Right. Damnit." Samus's eyes were drawn to the storm outside. Lindsey sighed along with her.

"The weather report says that the snow storm will have stopped by Friday morning. Meaning that the snow removal crews here will probably be done around then as well. So yay, we don't have to drive a rented car in the blizzard—just the aftermath of one. Which can still be frustrating, I know. So flip for it?"

Lindsey dug into her jeans pocket and displayed a quarter. She was already flipping it into the air before Samus could really respond to this new plan.

"Call it," Lindsey said, masking the identity of the coin on her palm. "Winner doesn't have to drive."

"Heads."

Lindsey revealed the coin. "Heads it is. Lucky you."

Samus let out a relief. "Oh, thank God."

"Well, we're still gonna flip for it on the way back. For now, I'll register the car with my card, and you can just forward me some cash?"

Samus nodded along to the rest of Lindsey's plans, making some notes as she did. By the end of an hour, their entire weekend was planned out in London. The conference started on Friday night and went to Sunday afternoon, but both Lindsey's and Samus's papers were supposed to be delivered on Saturday. That left Sunday for them to get home, and maybe sight-see, along with Friday night to maybe even socialize with academics.

"Only if there are drink vouchers, though," Lindsey stipulated. "You will not get me in a room full of academics without alcohol."

"Me too."

"You sure you're okay?" Lindsey asked after a

moment. She tilted her head to the side, her dark red lips pursed. "You've been really quiet."

"Don't worry. Just realized I still have to write the paper for the conference now."

"Ack. Me too. Shall we call it a day?"

Samus nodded, and after a few minutes, they were packed up and braving the snow outside the Grad House. When Lindsey went to turn off campus, towards the bus terminal, Samus lingered.

"You go ahead. I left some notes in my office."

"Okay. Message me tonight?"

"Always."

Lindsey blew Samus a kiss and walked away. Samus felt a subtle tingle that wasn't just from the cold. Lindsey, in spite of her overwhelming acceptance of Samus, was never into women. At first, it had confused Samus why someone as outgoing as Lindsey would want to hang around and not date, and it made her worry about her attractiveness as a woman, but she had learned to shrug those feelings off. Samus had been with a few boyfriends since then, but never any girlfriends—in spite of actively trying.

And now there's Jackie. Samus didn't really know what to do with a thought like that. Did she like Jackie in a romantic way? Or did she only want her to take the class so they could keep talking about what Le Guin was really trying to do with *The Left Hand of Darkness*? Even if Jackie was into queer texts, that didn't mean she was queer. Samus knew all of these things logically, but it still felt as if her head was spinning.

Once inside her office on campus, Samus shook out her scarf and scattered snow all over the carpet. No one else was around, making the empty cubicles seem eerily quiet. When she flicked on her computer, she went straight to her classes' online registration course. Only two students had dropped it since this morning, and they hadn't shown up, anyway, so Samus felt better. She allowed in two more students on the waitlist, but noticed that Jackie was neither one of those students.

Damn. I really thought she'd be into it. With a sigh, Samus tried to find the notes for her conference paper, but found herself going through her email archives. Since she often repeated the courses she taught, she had a solid list of standard feedback, old syllabi, and other correspondences. *If Jackie's been my student, that means I have...* Samus went through the year 2013, and after only a couple minutes of searching, found one of her students named Jacqueline.

Yikes. Her grade had barely been a 58. No wonder she hadn't continued on with English. The thought made Samus sad, especially since she was the one who'd done the grading. She absolutely hated giving shitty marks, and usually tried to avoid it at all costs. She pulled up one of Jackie's earlier assignments and gave it a quick skim read. It was a little rough around the edges—clearly something written the night before—but it wasn't bad. Not 58 bad. When Samus checked the grade, she realized she had given it a 72. *So why did everything go downhill?*

Samus searched through old files more and more. About halfway through that semester, Jackie had disappeared. She stopped handing in assignments, stopping commenting on people's posts online, and stopped doing anything. Then, a week before the final assignment was to be handed in, she emailed Samus in a panic.

> *Dear Prof. Mallory,*
>
> *I'm Jacqueline Vasquez from your ENGL 101 course. I'm so sorry, but I've been having family issues a lot this semester. I know I haven't submitted anything, and I'm willing to take the repercussions for that. But can I have an extension on the final assignment? I know if I just had more time, I could hand it in, and it would be better.*
>
> *Thanks for your consideration.*
> *Sincerely,*
> *Jacqueline Vasquez*
> *0542897*

The email was something Samus saw all the time. Over the years, she had learned to craft a very standard response to messages like these, sometimes allowing the extension based on prior correspondence, and other times forwarding the issue to the supervisor of the course to deal with. But as she read her response now, she realized it wasn't a form letter. In fact, it was downright mean.

> *No. I cannot give extensions to you because it wouldn't be fair to others. Perhaps if you had come to me earlier, this issue could have been avoided. Now, since there's no way to verify you claim, I can't allow an extension. Besides, you have three more days until the due date. I'm sure you can write something in that amount of time and hand it in. Handing in something is better than nothing.*

Samus shirked back at the response. She closed all the windows and leaned back in her chair, utterly embarrassed by her former behaviour. *I was in a bad mood, and I made Jackie suffer for it.* Waves of guilt washed over her. Years later, Samus could see so clearly what was going on and what had happened. She had just come out as trans, just started transitioning, and she deliberately taught online classes so her awkward in-between physical appearance wasn't broadcasted to the public. She was dealing with name change forms and the passport office to get everything swapped over, while also going to therapy and trying to get her hormones renewed every month.

And by the end of that semester, when Jackie had emailed with her own excuses, Samus had reached her limit. She didn't care about her students anymore, especially if they had "personal issues," because all Samus had been doing that semester was going through personal issues, and she still showed up. She still got her work done. She had nearly failed Jackie to make a point and not granted her an extension because Samus had felt as if no one—except Lindsey—had cared about her.

That was wrong. Samus could see that so clearly now. When she thought about how she had basically made Jackie afraid of taking another English course, when she was clearly so into fantasy literature, she felt even worse.

Goddamnit. Samus had known transitioning would be difficult, and her "past self" would come back to haunt her. But she thought that it would be Mark, not Samus, she would try to hide and forget about. *But you can make mistakes no matter who you are. And this was definitely a mistake.*

Samus logged out of her email server, then stared at a blank word document. She tried to type the title for her conference paper, but made two typos in as many words. *Not now.* There was no way she was going to even attempt the rest of the work she had today.

Instead, she found Jackie's last name and wrote it down, along with her other contact info. Maybe, just maybe, Samus could make things right.

Chapter Three

"The blizzard's getting bad out there."

"What?" Though Jackie moved the mic away from her mouth, she didn't bother to turn around and properly address Alicia. Her eyes remained glued to her screen and her avatar in front of her. Why was Alicia in her room, anyway? It was still afternoon. "I'm kinda busy right now. Aren't you supposed to be at work?"

"At work? It's seven at night, Jack. Have you been online since I left? In the same spot?"

"Umm..." Jackie bit her lip as her avatar climbed over a barricade only to get shot. The body fell down onto the dirt and her screen went red. Voices from her other gamers sighed and groaned. When the cursing began, she took out the headphones from her ears and logged off completely.

"Leesha, you made me screw up."

Alicia folded her hands across her chest, raising her eyebrows. "Oh, no. You can't pin this on me."

"Well, what do you want then? Since you've clearly broken into my room for a purpose."

Alicia huffed. "Your door was open, so I figured you wanted to plan. We still have to find a car, Jackie. With all this snow, that's not an easy thing."

"I know, I know. I have been thinking about the con. I've just... been distracted. Time kinda slipped by me."

"I can tell. Since you never really answered me, I'm going to assume that you really haven't gotten up from your computer since I left for the salon. Which is fine, but let's get undistracted now. We still need to plan our costumes, pack, and plan make-up. We're driving out tomorrow night, and I'll be at work all day, so this is our only time..."

"I know, Leesha. Please. Just let me think for a minute?"

Alicia seemed to hear the hitch in Jackie's voice. She uncrossed her arms with a sympathetic nod. "Do you want me to order a pizza? That may go a long way. I'm going to do that."

When Alicia left, Jackie let out a low breath. She loved Alicia. *Really*. They'd been best friends since high school and became roommates when they both left for university. Even when Alicia dropped out of Waterloo U and went to cosmetology school, they stayed in the same apartment while Alicia commuted to the college down the road. Now, as Jackie was finishing up her degree in math, Alicia was already in a full time position at the local salon in the mall. It wasn't the glamorous life they had first dreamed up when they were sixteen and desperate to leave their small town, but Jackie liked where they had ended up a lot.

Especially when they went to cons. The con this weekend had been in the works for months and they were going all-out. This particular event was a small gathering specifically devoted to many non-collectable card games developed by a company called Soda Pop Corporation. Non-collectable basically meant that instead of getting randomized cards (like in *Magic: The Gathering*), a non-collectable card game meant that Soda Pop Corp released regular expansions that contained a set amount of cards. Each time Alicia or Jackie picked up an expansion, they knew what was in the deck. There was no bartering for the "best" cards, or out-bidding someone like they so often saw at *Magic: The Gathering* games. Instead, all card games released by Soda Pop Corp were about playing with cards *and* telling a good story. That was part of the reason why they loved Soda Pop's cards so much; they were small universes that they—and especially Jackie—could lose themselves in for days on end. Jackie's recent obsession was a cyberpunk game called *Hack the Planet*, which was basically a feminist version of every single sci-fi movie made in the 90s involving hackers. Alicia had only just started to get the hang of *Hack the Planet* after Jackie had showed her how to play two months ago, so she'd been thrilled when Alicia finally agreed to cosplay as characters from the game this weekend.

"Pizza's ordered," Alicia said as she came back into the room. She flopped down on Jackie's bed, just under her *Evangelion* poster and right next to her *My Neighbour Totoro* plushie. Alicia picked up the toy and made it dance across her belly, before she curled a hand through her hair. "What do we need to talk about first?"

"I called the car rental place yesterday, and they're out of cars."

"How can you be out of cars? That seems like a bad business model."

"They're out of ones we can drive, I mean. All they have left is a moving truck and it's two times the price. Plus, you know, driving a rig like that in the winter is asking for death."

"Shit. I'm not taking the Greyhound bus to London. Can you imagine cosplay on the bus? It will be another Anime North snafu. Never again, *senpai*. I've learned my lesson. Never again."

Jackie chuckled a bit at the memory. When her phone buzzed in her pocket, she flinched.

"What was that?" Alicia asked, noticing Jackie's aversion right away. "Who are you avoiding?"

"Who do you think?"

"Right. Mommy dearest." Alicia snickered, then her face grew bright. "What if...?"

"No. No. And no. I'm not asking my mom for her car."

"Why not?" Alicia whined. "We need one. She'll let us have it. And she may even give us gas money, Jackie. You have to call and ask. Especially since the car rental place is out of cars."

Jackie sighed. She really, really didn't want to admit that Alicia was right. Her mother would let them take the car without a second thought, and chip in on the trip's expenses. Right now, Jackie's mother was probably only texting to wish Jackie a happy early birthday and to tell her that she loved her. *Oh such terrible things,* Jackie thought bitterly. *So why am I afraid of it?* Her relationship with her mother had been complicated ever since Jackie had come out as gay a few years ago. But whose relationship with their mother wasn't complicated? Alicia had to deal with the same flack from her parents when she came out a bi, but Alicia's mother was far more aggressive about it. Jackie' mom just felt... smothering. It was hard to describe, so Jackie didn't bother complaining about it to anyone but Alicia. But even that wasn't really working, especially when Alicia knew Jackie's mom almost as well as her own.

"Jackie? You there?" Alicia asked.

"Yes... I'm just..."

"What?" Alicia challenged. Her winged eyeliner and tight black jeans made her look so intimidating in that moment. "I know you and your mom aren't the best people to have in the same room together, but we're not talking about an awkward Christmas dinner. We're talking about seeing your mom for fifteen minutes while we pick up the car. What's so bad about that?"

"A lot of things."

"But in context, not many. You know?" When Jackie didn't answer, Alicia huffed again. "I'll come. You know that, right? I can even do all the talking."

Jackie considered this. Her phone buzzed in her pocket again, along with the doorbell. Alicia rose to her feet but stared menacingly at Jackie as she left the room. "Think about it. Answer those texts. Or no pizza."

Jackie's stomach rumbled. She lost all track of time when she was gaming. She flipped open her phone and opened the messages from her mother. Ignoring most of the chit-chat, Jackie went right to the point.

Hey, thanks for the early wishes. We're good here. Alicia and I are taking a trip this weekend. I know, it's a blizzard right now but we know where we're going. Can we borrow the car this weekend? I can return it with the same amount of gas and whatever else you need. Thanks!

"Ugh, there. I was kind and courteous and sent the message," Jackie said as soon as Alicia came back into the room. She set a box of pizza on Jackie's bed, grabbing a slice of pizza for herself. "Can I have some now?"

"I suppose. Thanks, by the way. I really appreciate you asking. With the cash we'll save, I'll buy you some merch."

"You know the way to my heart." Jackie grabbed a slice of pizza and sat across from Alicia on her bed. They chatted back and forth, planning some of their route to London and back, looking at the program online, before Jackie's mother got back to them.

Of course, sweetheart. You're my daughter and anything you want. Don't worry about gas, just stop by early so we can talk and catch up.

"Ugh," Jackie said. "There you go. I've sold my soul, but there you go."

Alicia furrowed her brows as she skimmed Jackie's phone. "I see no anger or animosity in this text. I don't understand."

"It's just... overwhelming. I don't know. She's always so... clingy. I mean—stop by early and chat? What am I even supposed to say?"

"You're her kid. I don't think being clingy counts. Say anything. She'll be grateful."

"I know, but I feel as if she's trying to be my best friend and not my mom, you know? And that fucks me up, because she has too much power in the relationship to ever be my friend. I guess, anyway."

Alicia shrugged. "I'd take a best friend mom over an enemy mom anyway."

"I know, sorry," Jackie said. "I really should stop complaining."

"No, no. That's not what I meant. It's just... I think everyone has a fucked up relationship with their parents at some point in time. And twenties are rife with that. Maybe we'll get over it as we age, or as they age and realize we're the ones taking care of them when they reach the golden years."

"I hope it's sooner than that," Jackie said, surprised by how much she meant it. "Especially in time for graduation."

"Oooh, exciting! Will you let me make your gown?"

"I don't think that's how it works."

"Spoil sport." Alicia took a bite of pizza and winked. "So let's focus on our costumes now. You've been working on mine, right?"

With the topic switched, Jackie felt more at home. Opening her dresser drawer, she pulled out the bundle of fabric and supplies that made up her cosplay tool box. Her sewing machine was in the closet, ready to use to finish up a few seams on

Alicia's outfit.

"I tried to make it so you looked more like someone from the *Matrix* and less like someone from *Lollypop Chainsaw*," Jackie said as she handed over the brightly coloured fabric. Alicia made an O with her mouth in pleasure then held up the top to her chest. Jackie could already see where she'd have to take out some of the fabric and readjust to Alicia's breasts, which Jackie never seemed to be able to fit right when she sewed for Alicia. She used to blame it on Alicia's weight fluctuating so much in high school, but Jackie knew that it was her own carelessness. She wrote down people's measurements and then lost them after each session.

"Ugh, I'm sorry," Jackie apologized. "I figured I'd need to fix it, so don't worry, I've budgeted time and fabric and—"

"I like it. Really, I do. I can see where it'll all come together."

Jackie beamed. *Hack the Planet* was a cyberpunk game, and Alicia was set to go as one of the main hackers, Max. The characters had circuits for hair, which Alicia insisted she could do with curlers and some silver highlights. Her costume was skin tight, with green—almost Dayglo—colour around the abdomen and over the thighs. The rest of the material was grey, but supposed to look futuristic, like a robot. Alicia's make-up and circuit hair would definitely make the costume come together.

"Good. I'm so glad you like it."

"Do you need to take my measurements again

before we continue?" Alicia asked, dropping her voice an octave. She wiggled her brows and played up her flirtations.

"Probably, actually. That's the safest bet with me. But I just your measurements, don't worry."

"What, me worry?" Alicia laughed as she bounced off the bed. She held her arms above her head as Jackie got her measuring tape to figure out her bust size, along with her shoulder size. Alicia kept her shirt on while this was done, since the shirt was skin-tight anyway. Once Jackie had gathered the numbers, she told Alicia she was set.

"Yikes," Alicia said. She rubbed under her bra line, where Jackie knew she'd probably have bright red marks. "I wish I could get a breast reduction. Maybe I should."

"I wish I could too, really."

"But yours are like... A cups. What problem could they be?"

Jackie shrugged, feeling blush etch across her cheeks. "They get in the way when I cosplay guys."

"Yeah, but surgery for cosplay? Now that's dedication. "

"I've seen people do it. Remember that one woman from Montreal? That was a breast enlargement, but still... It's been done."

"Whatever. I think you look good as you are, Jack."

Alicia slumped on the bed, the conversation over to her. While she rooted through her make-up and hair accessories, Jackie made the technical adjustments to Alicia's costume. Jackie fell easily into her "zone" while working. She used to think that video games were the only place she could really let go and forget about everything, but once she had finally shelled out the money for a proper sewing machine, she had realized the potential for forgetting here, too. As soon as her hands touched the machine, she could already feel the vibration and hear the gentle noises it made. And she always felt *so* much more in control of what was going on. She could literally make—and then unmake—something and know exactly what she was doing.

"Here you go." After working for a while, Jackie held up the new shirt. Not much had changed, but when Alicia shimmied into it, they could both see the difference. Now it hugged her body in all the right ways.

Alicia squealed in delight. "I love it. Now with my make-up, and I'll really look like Max."

"Totally. You'll steal the show."

"We have to get pictures at the con," Alicia stated. "Okay?"

"Definitely."

"Who are you going to be again? Another hacker like me?"

Jackie shrugged. "I don't know, actually."

"You don't know? We've been planning this for months!"

Again, Jackie shrugged. Each time she thought she had a person to play, she would start to make the costume and then lose interest. The hackers were the best characters in *Hack the Planet*, but none of them were men. There were a couple other doctors and business people in the world who were men (or androgynous-looking), but who really wanted to play something so ordinary? Part of the allure of the game was the world-building it had done and the separate factions it had built up. The Hackers were the underdogs and the heroes of the game, but there were also the commune workers who were hippies living off the grid in the middle of a desert, the nine-to-fivers who had normal jobs and sometimes committed horrible crimes or saved the day, and the corporate execs who were often viewed by fans as the true antagonists. When people played the game, they often picked a "side" to be on and built their deck of characters around the goals and objectives of their faction. Who won depended on the cards and the skill of the player. And Jackie *really* liked the Hackers. She'd been playing them non-stop for months now. Moving on from their wacky dyed hair and silver suits to the plain nine-to-fivers or even the white robes of the communes seemed awful.

When Jackie explained her reservations to Alicia, Alicia tsk-tsked

"Can't you make up a cool guy?"

"What?"

"Like a hacker guy? I'm sure there are men hackers. I mean, why wouldn't there be? We just haven't been issued the cards yet."

"Maybe... but I don't want to dress up as an OC. The point of cosplaying at an event like this is to get people to recognize you, you know?"

"You're so difficult." Alicia grabbed the deck of

Hack the Planet cards she kept in her make-up kit. She flicked through them at warp speed, discarding most of the deck before she finally gasped. "That's it. You can be Julian Howard."

Jackie squinted as she went over her ever-expanding card collection in her mind. She came up with nothing. "Who?"

"The villain! Well, one of them. See?" She handed over the card.

Jackie recognized it right away. "Oh, you mean The Postman!"

"Yeah! Is that his nickname? I don't watch as many YouTube videos as you, so you'll forgive me if I can't catch up. But he's perfect, right? One of the lesser known villains, part of the corporation who works at a TV company like Fox. He has bright red hair and a green suit. You're like the Dayglo Walt Disney or Rupert Murdoch."

"Gross."

"But cool, right? You can make a suit in a few days, can't you?"

"Umm..." Jackie *could*. She had made harder projects in less time. She took the card from Alicia's hands, staring at the guy's wardrobe and coifed hair. Almost no one liked to play him in the game, since he wasn't the best villain. Whenever someone did play him, everyone called him The Postman because he often just showed up and shot everything—he went postal. So not the best skills set, either.

But he did have a lot of colours. His suit, although really weird, would be an interesting challenge.

"Come on," Alicia encouraged. "You would be so good as him."

"Really? Even if my hair and skin is like ten times darker than his?"

"So? That only means I get to cut and style it, right?"

"*What?*" Jackie coughed.

"Come on! Let me cut your hair short and dye it. I know we'd normally get wigs or something, but I actually think you'd look cool with orange hair."

"Really?" Jackie glanced towards her closet door with a full length mirror on it. Her dark hair was at her shoulders, but that was mostly out of laziness rather than style. She could get used to having short hair like she did in high school. But orange hair? "What if it looks ridiculous?"

"So you're like that for a weekend and then you change back."

Alicia stood, made her way behind Jackie and ran fingers through her hair. Already, Jackie could feel how skilled Alicia had gotten. She trusted her—both as her best friend, and as a stylist. When Jackie looked down at the card again, she zeroed in on Julian Howard's tie, which was speckled with cat heads. *Okay, now I'm sold.*

"So what do you say?" Alicia asked a moment later.

"Yeah. Go for it."

~~*

Three hours later Jackie was sitting on the

bathroom counter. She couldn't stop staring at her hair. The orange was practically neon under the harsh bathroom lights. She'd only keep this colour for the weekend and then dye it back to good ol' faithful black.

But the short hair. It made her feel so, so much better. This feeling was more than just getting it off her neck and away from her eyes each and every time she looked down. This sudden relief was different. She ran her fingers through the hair at the back, and marveled at how short it all was. So *nice*. She couldn't even really articulate why. It didn't seem to matter. *So long as I like it, I'm set.*

She stayed in the bathroom a little while longer. Alicia had invited over her quasi-boyfriend after finishing up with the hair, and the two of them were watching Netflix on the couch in the living room. Jackie could hear the theme song for *Orange is the New Black* and then their raucous laughter every so often. Normally, Jackie would have gone out and joined them. *Alicia's probably worried that I hate everything she's done to me.* But Jackie just... needed time to appreciate this a little while longer.

As she waited, she scrolled through suit plans on her phone. She technically had a class tomorrow, but she already knew she'd be skipping it in favour of working on his multi-coloured wreck of a suit all day. When she found the perfect pattern, she noted that the model had used tweed for the pattern. Jackie was drawn to it but couldn't figure out why. There was no character who ever wore tweed that she'd want to cosplay. Still, she added the suit plan to her bookmarks for later. She was just about to leave the bathroom when her phone buzzed again. She tightened her grip on it reflexively, anticipating her mother, but was surprised to see an email from Samus Mallory.

Hi Jackie,

Please don't freak out, but I found your old email through my course records. I just wanted to let you know that I can add you to the wait list for the class. There are two people ahead of you, but you never know, right?
You totally don't have to take my class, but I do want you to know that I enjoyed talking with you today. It made me a lot less nervous before lecturing—so thank you for that.

Take care,
Samus (or Sam, whatever, I'm not picky)

Jackie furrowed her brows. How weird and delightful. She was halfway through typing a response when there was a knock at the door.

"Jackie...?" Alicia asked, her voice tense. "You've been in there a really long time. Are you dying? Please tell me I can still have your mom's car if you're dying."

"I'm not dying, just..." Jackie caught her reflection in the mirror. For a minute, she didn't look like Jackie—the reflection she had come to know and accept for more of her life. She didn't look like Julian Howard, either, the mega-conglomerate billionaire from *Hack the Planet*. She looked likes someone she hadn't met before. "I'm fine. Just getting suit plans."

"Really? Okay, that's a relief. Well, can you do that in your room, because I really need to pee."

"Sorry. Coming."

Jackie left the bathroom and said a quick hello to Darren before she went into her bedroom. Her heart pounded when she saw the sewing machine, but she didn't have any of the proper colour fabric to continue making anything. She set an alarm for eight in the morning, so she could go out to FabricLand. When she noticed the half-finished email, she sighed. What did she really want to say to Samus? She wasn't really sure. She hardly remembered her from English 101, and really, she didn't want to remember much of that year to begin with.

So, for the rest of the night, Jackie played her video game, the message unsent.

Chapter Four

"You ready to go?"

Lindsey stood in the middle of their hotel room, a hand on her hip. She looked amazing in her a-line skirt and a dark blue blouse. It was almost a shame that she'd have to put a coat on in order to get to the conference at the university a little over fifteen minutes away.

"I'm almost done," Samus said. She sighed when she looked at herself in the mirror. She wasn't competing with Lindsey—why would she?—but she couldn't help but feel a little inferior and definitely in her shadow. Estrogen had softened her features tremendously, around her cheeks in particular, and emphasized her heart-shaped face. Her thin ginger hair had been the bane of her existence for a long time. She wanted to have long, flowing hair the way Lindsey did—but years of testosterone affecting her already fine locks made that impossible. So Samus had finally opted for a shorter hair style that swooped to the side, giving her added volume while still remaining distinctly feminine. But even now, Samus adjusted her bangs in the mirror obsessively.

"You look beautiful," Lindsey stated. "Seriously. And the whole blouse-cardigan combination? Love it."

The Big Reveal

Samus's green blouse and black cardigan were both loose, allowing for her new curves to fill out even more. Her breasts were already a B cup, and they would probably keep growing. She loved the new softness to her body, but sometimes it was difficult to find tops in a big enough size. The green one was a standard at this point in time, along with her black dress pants and green flats.

"Thank you!"

"I know academics aren't supposed to care that much about what we're wearing," Lindsey went on, rolling her eyes a bit, "but they do. And I feel much better when I get up there to talk when I'm coordinated. Like my own private uniform, almost. So, do I look okay, too?"

"Yes, of course! Always, Linds," Samus said. "Sorry, I've been inside my own head this morning. I didn't mean to neglect you."

Lindsey waved it off. "S'okay. Just nerves? Or is there another reason you're trapped in your own head?"

Samus paused a bit longer than she should have. Lindsey noticed the slight apprehension.

"You know what? Tell me afterwards with some drinks. We really gotta go. Registration is happening in ten minutes, and I want to eat all the free muffins I can before we go on."

"Right. Sorry. I still need to put on eyeliner. You want to bring around the car?"

Lindsey huffed, but Samus knew it was mostly for show. Lindsey gave a quick wave before she left the hotel room and Samus finished putting on her make-up. She also checked her phone, for the hundredth time since she sent Jackie the message, and shook her head. *Stupid move. Rookie move. Just because someone is a nerd like you doesn't mean they're gonna like you, too.* Wasn't that the lesson of *500 Days of Summer*? And here Samus was, still thinking the way Hollywood movies depicted romance life was true.

"I really gotta get my shit together," Samus said aloud, then leaned in close to finish her eyeliner. When she managed to somehow keep her hands steady, she smiled. At least she could master some things.

She checked to make sure her hotel key and conference paper were in her bag one last time before she stepped out of the hotel room. She had to hurry to the other end of the hallway to make it on time to the elevator.

"Hold it, please?" Samus called out.

A hand came out and wedged itself between the elevator doors. Samus walked up and stepped inside. "Thank you!"

"No problem."

Samus baulked for a second at the person with her. They had bright orange hair—orange like the fruit, not like Samus's ginger hair—and wore a neon-coloured suit. And was that a tie with cats on it? When they spoke, though, their voice was high-pitched.

Are they here for the con? Samus wondered. She had seen a sign when she and Lindsey had pulled into the hotel late last night about some kind of gaming convention. She was usually too focused on her own stuff just before a conference, but the con pulled her in because she had never heard of the game before. Lindsey hadn't either, and really, that had been the extent of the conversation before they fell into bed exhausted.

When Samus realized she was staring at the stranger, she turned away. She watched as the hotel floor numbers went from four to three, waiting out some of the tension. It seemed worse than usual after only a couple seconds of silence. Samus was about to grasp her cell phone to call Lindsey or hit her panic button, when the person spoke again.

"Samus?"

Samus turned, her panic rising. "Yeah? How did you...?"

"It's me, Jackie."

"Oh." Samus let out a breath, nearly dropping her phone as she did. She squinted at Jackie's orange hair; she could see some of the dark roots now and recognized her facial structure and brown skin from before. "Oh, I'm so sorry. You completely startled me."

"I didn't mean to. Sorry. I know it's a bit weird—not to mention really embarrassing—seeing me like this." Jackie gestured to her suit and then to her hair.

"I admit it was a bit of a surprise. Are you at the con?"

"Yeah, I am. Are you?"

Samus couldn't ignore the way Jackie's eyes lit up with that prospect. Samus gestured to her blouse and her conference paper in her hand. "Not quite. A different kind of dress up for me today."

"Oh? What are you doing?"

"I'm giving a paper at Western University. Just on video games and gender politics. My friend Lindsey is going too. But on Virginia Woolf and gender politics."

"Oh, really? I bet that's fun."

"Oh yeah, totally," Samus said, unsure if Jackie's enthusiasm was real or not. She decided to go on as if it was genuine. "As you can probably guess, the whole conference is on gender theory. I figured it would be less risky giving a conference paper on gaming here, rather than at a game studies conference, but I anticipate getting some really angry questions from male gamers, anyway. Maybe that's why I'm so nervous."

Samus tried to laugh a bit, but it came out a breathy sigh. The elevator doors pinged and the foyer light washed inside. A few people buzzed around the front desk, and Samus noted the red Mazda she and Lindsey had rented idling at the front.

"Aw, really? I'm sorry you're already anticipating criticism. I hope you do well," Jackie said as they both stepped out of the elevator. Jackie lingered alongside Samus, though her eyes flitted down the hallway where more people dressed in neon costumes hovered by a conference hall doorway.

"Thank you. If I don't do well, though, it's not a big deal. The conference gives us alcohol vouchers since there was a group rate for us at this hotel. Alcohol saves the day each time."

"That's great. They should start doing that

here."

"Well..." Samus didn't want to go, though she had a feeling Lindsey was going to start angry-texting her soon. Or worse—start honking. "I hope you have fun at your con. I've never heard of these games before, so it's really neat to see some aspect of it like this up close."

"You've never played? Really?"

"No. I guess grad school has ruined my interest in new games unless I can add it to my dissertation."

"That sucks. But your conference doesn't go all night, does it?"

"No..."

"Then I could tell you about *Hack the Planet*. Maybe even play a game? If you want, of course. No pressure. I'm just..." Jackie stopped, running a hand through her still distractingly orange hair. "I just like playing and I feel bad I didn't reply to your email."

"Don't. Oh my God, I felt bad I even sent it."

"Don't." Jackie smiled. "I was busy making this, so I ignored all my obligations."

When Jackie tugged on her suit, Samus gasped. "You made that? Amazing."

"It's a bit of a specialty by now. I also made my friend Alicia's cosplay."

Samus followed Jackie's gaze over to a different woman in a skin-tight costume with neon colours around the thighs. Her hair looked to have silver pipe cleaners in it, forming sparks or circuits, she wasn't quite sure. *A friend?* Samus wondered. *Or something more?* She tried not to linger too much there.

"That's really cool," Samus said. "I might have to enlist your services to help fix some of my clothing. But I have to go now. Conference. And such..."

"Yeah. Of course. You have my email, but let me send you my number, okay? I was serious about the game."

"Okay, sure." Samus smiled. Her phone vibrated in her pocket, but she knew that couldn't be Jackie already. Definitely Lindsey; she had to hurry. "I look forward to it. I'll see you around, okay?"

Jackie waved before she walked down the opposite hallway and disappeared into a convention room. Samus was still shaken by how different Jackie looked—but also how different she acted. She was so much more confident and forthright. She barely stuttered or mumbled. *And her smile.* She smiled so much more then. Samus chalked it all up to the cosplay and being more in her element. The invitation to a game still made Samus's heart pound with excitement, but she couldn't get too far ahead of herself. As soon as she got into the car with Lindsey, the anxiety of presenting came back.

"What was all that about? You took *forever*," Lindsey complained. "I mean, you look great, so I suppose it was worth it. But give me more warning next time?"

"Sorry. But thanks," Samus said, still beaming. "I think I really needed to hear that."

"Well, relax. We're almost there."

Most of the snow had been ploughed, so their drive would be a lot easier. *And we won't even be late.* Already, her day was going much better than she anticipated.

Chapter Five

"Just one more picture," David said. He held the camera in front of him, angling precisely so he didn't disturb his styled hair as he put his face next to the lens again.

"A group shot?" Alicia asked. "Or one by one?"

"One more group shot, then I want to do some individual shot so you guys can re-enact your cards. You know?"

"What about you?" Alicia teased. "When are you going to show off your effort?"

"That's what tripods and timers are for, my dear."

"Ew. Don't call me that. I'm done with boys."

Some conversation from other cosplayers erupted as Alicia clarified her new single lifestyle. *Well, Darren didn't last long*, Jackie thought as she scratched at her tie. On the drive down, Alicia had gone over the pros and cons of that relationship, but Jackie had somehow missed the actual break-up in all of that. She shrugged it away and readied her pose. David set up his tripod with a timer then shifted into the group shot. The chatter died down as everyone waited for the camera's sudden flash burst.

"We're done now? We're free to move?" Michelle stated.

David nodded. "For now, yeah. Thank you guys for being patient."

Michelle let out a relieved sigh. She was dressed as yet another hacker called Bex. Her suit, Jackie noted with a hint of pride, wasn't as precisely put together as Alicia's. Ever since setting into the con, Alicia received compliment after compliment on her outfit, all of which she directly passed onto Jackie. Jackie wasn't quite sure if it was Alicia's body or Jackie's craftsmanship being praised, but it didn't matter, really, since they both benefited from the kind words. People also seemed to like Jackie's costume; when she and Alicia did the preliminary walkthrough of the con, a few groups ran up to both of them and shouted "the postman!" at the top of their lungs before disappearing.

Now, it was already mid-afternoon and they were finalizing their photo shoot with David. He was a friend of a friend, not really well known to Jackie, but she liked his work. He made all five of them who were dressed up as characters from *Hack the Planet* squish together, placing Jackie at the back since she was super-tall and the villain. His photography skills sometimes reminded her of an elementary class photo, but she knew the work would look super professional by the time he uploaded it to Flickr and Facebook—even the shot when he added himself to the front last minute.

"So, now I want to move on to shoot you all like the individual cards. Jackie, you wanna go first?"

"The postman!" Michelle and Becky shouted

and clapped. As Jackie walked along, she pretended she really was Julian Howard and was doing her victory strut.

"Okay, how about you sit down at one of the tables? We can add some of your tools from the card, too, and strike the pose he's making on the image. You think?"

Jackie pulled out the card from the deck. Julian Howard sat in a giant CEO office with a window in the background that showed the cyberpunk city at night. In front of him sat a tablet and a teddy bear. Jackie grabbed her cell phone to use as a replacement for the tablet and borrowed the plushie Becky had recently purchased to replace the teddy bear.

As she sat down, Jackie did her best to smile and enjoy the photo session, even as David kept telling her to move "just a smidge" to the right at least six times. He showed her some of the images between the shots and though she still felt awkward having her picture taken, she liked these a lot better than maybe all of her high school photos combined.

"That's great," she said to David at the final image. "Thanks so much."

"Not at all. You should give me your number so I can send them to you."

"Oh?" Jackie said. "Why not email?"

"That too, sure. I was thinking number so, I could, uh, call you about making me a suit, maybe?

"Oh." Jackie beamed them. "Sure. I'd love to."

She traded numbers with David before he

called Alicia up for her session. Alicia winked at Jackie as she walked by her, and then began to pose. Most of Alicia's shots were with one of the ray guns she had fashioned out of an old super soaker. During the photo shoot, Jackie added David's number to her phone. Her mind swarmed with all the potential sewing projects she could bring in. Maybe she could even start a business? She had gotten so used to keeping her cosplay a secret all throughout high school, and only making the select item for Alicia during university, that the thought of really going public gave her goose bumps.

I knew there was a reason I said yes to cons. I knew it. Other than the full-on geeking out and fun she often had at cons, there was the social aspect she often ignored. She had grown so used to keeping Alicia by her side at all times, like a sidekick duo, she completely forgot that there were other people in the world who were just as awesome. *And that think you're awesome, too.*

Like Samus. Jackie switched over to Samus's email and phone number in her phone. She didn't have time to message before Alicia came back.

"What was that?" Alicia asked, nudging her shoulder.

"What was what?"

"With David! Did you give him your number?"

"Yes. Because of the photos. He's going to commission me to make him a suit."

"Oh, is he now?" Alicia narrowed her eyes and shook her head. "Please tell me you're not this naive."

"What?"

"O, my sweet summer child." Alicia put her arm around Jackie and held her close. Jackie pried herself away, not liking the tone in Alicia's voice.

"What? Why *wouldn't* he want me to make something? I'm good. You keep getting compliments, and I made this and..."

"Sweetie, no. I wasn't insulting your work. You're great. Of course you are. And maybe David does want a suit done. The stuff he's wearing now is kind of dreadful. But he also wants to bang."

"What? Ugh."

"Come on. You haven't noticed this about cons yet? Everyone at these places wants to bang. It's the 'same time next year' kind of deal. You meet nerds who are into the same nerdy things you are, and you're all on some kind of vacation. There's no pressure, no stakes. So of course, it's time to fuck."

"Right, of course. I should always listen to you, sex guru Leesha."

Jackie tried to act appalled, when really, she just felt foolish. Of course that's what David had been doing. She wasn't an idiot. She had gone to a dozen renaissance faires and hooked up with a dozen elves and fairy girls. She even had a pretty intense relationship with someone she met at Anime North for a couple months afterwards. But those always seemed like isolated incidents, just her luck that day, and romantic trysts. Not fucking for the sake of fucking.

And not David, of all people. Jackie shuddered. "Does he even know I'm only into women?"

Alicia shrugged. "Probably not. Want me to let him down for you?"

Jackie watched as David chatted up Michelle during the middle of their photo shoot. She thought she saw them exchange numbers, then sighed. "You know what? Go ahead. I can't even really face him right now."

"Hey, it's not a big deal. Everyone does it. Relax, okay? The day is far from done." Alicia squeezed Jackie's shoulder before approaching David again. She waited until Michelle's set was done, then seemed to get into a heated conversation. When Jackie couldn't watch anymore, she turned her attention back to her phone.

A message from Samus popped up right away. *So... not many Gamer Guys here. I think I'm safe from being called names. I actually got some really interesting questions about the paper.*

That's great! I think all the regressive nerds ended up here.

That's a shame, Samus replied. *Are you not having fun?*

Jackie sighed. She was having fun. Really. Even with this David miscommunication, she was really enjoying herself. But as she looked at the planner for the rest of the day, she realized none of it appealed anymore.

Yeah, it's good. Lots of fun—I just finished a photo shoot, which was neat, especially since I normally hate photos but these came out okay. But I think I may be tapped for the day.

Maybe you need to change out of the neon

suit. I know I need to change out of my dress-up for the day. I'm craving jeans and T-shirts so much right now.

Does that mean you're heading back to the hotel? Jackie asked. Her eyes flitted towards the conference door, as if she expected Samus to be there already.

Soon. Lindsey wants to talk to one last prof, then we're gonna get out and into human clothing, I think. Linds may want to head back to the uni after changing though, which leaves me alone. You still want to play the game? Or are you gamed out for the day?

I think I'm gamed out. But I'll hang out, if you want. Maybe we can talk about Le Guin? Or something. Doesn't matter.

Sure. What else would I save my drink tickets for?

Jackie smiled down at her phone. Already, her mood was shifting. She glanced up to notice Michelle and Alicia talking very closely, possibly both bonding over David's aggressive flirting. David was done with the photo shoot, and now at the other end of the con, talking to another woman in a skimpy cosplay outfit. In that moment, Jackie noticed how everyone seemed to be with a partner of some kind. *Wow, maybe there was something in the air at cons. Hook-up central.* But Jackie knew exactly where she'd prefer to be.

Okay, great. Just give me ten minutes to clean up and then I'll meet you in the lobby.

Sounds perfect.

Chapter Six

"I do really want to play that game," Samus said. "Eventually."

"Sure. Of course. I really like it, but thanks for putting it off." Jackie smiled.

The two of them were stationed at the hotel bar, where Samus used two of her drink tickets so they could both get a beer. Samus was dressed in jeans and T-shirt like she said, but her shirt had a woman with big, muscular arms on it, posed as a cyberpunk Rosie The Riveter with the words 'we can do it' written above. Jackie loved the image, even if it made her simple black Fall Out Boy T-shirt seem a bit ridiculous by comparison. Samus also wore a cardigan, and when she rolled up the sleeves slightly, Jackie swore she saw a tattoo peaking out near her forearm.

"So," Samus said. "I know I asked in a text, but how is your con going? I had a feeling there may be something you didn't or couldn't write down."

"Nah, not really. I mean—I love cons, but I think my friend Alicia is the social butterfly who gets everyone she sets her sights on. I'm pretty sure she broke up with her quasi-boyfriend on the way here, and is now talking to a new girl." Jackie pressed her lips together, realizing how awkward all of that sounded. Was this even a date? *Ugh.*

Don't focus on it. "I also think I just want my hair to go back to normal. Orange like this makes me stick out like a pylon."

Samus chuckled. "It suits you, actually. Not the orange, but the short cut."

"Really?" Jackie ran her hands along the back of her neck, still relishing the closed-cropped feel. "Thanks. I like your T-shirt, by the way."

"Oh." Samus glanced down, blushing slightly. "Thank you. Have you ever played *Metroid*?"

"No. I haven't played any new games in a while. But I'll look it up. I sometimes watch game reviews online, so maybe I've come across it before."

"Maybe! But if you start playing, you gotta start with the 1986 version. Tell me what you think when you find it, okay?"

Jackie nodded then took a sip of her drink. The excitement and chatter from before dissipated. Now the silence was tense, and though Jackie thought it was just herself being awkward, she could see the subtle tremble in Samus's fingers. *Fuck. Maybe we should have brought the game. That way, we could focus on something else when silence happens like this.*

"How's your class going?" Jackie asked, trying to ask something neutral. "Maybe I can teach you the game and you can show it to your students?"

"Maybe, actually," Samus said. "I've only had a few sessions so far, but I'm enjoying it. I think I may have been too bold putting D&D down as something to study, even if the Monster Manuel reads as its own fantasy text. So maybe... *Hack the*

Planet? Is that what it's called?"

"Yes, *Hack the Planet*. It's cyberpunk, so not fantasy, but still speculative lit, in a way."

"Totally. Maybe it could work."

The silence returned. Jackie wanted to scream. Why was everything always so much easier over the computer or phone? Ugh. Jackie spotted Alicia heading to the elevator with Michelle, a hand on the small of her back. There went her room for the next couple hours. Jackie couldn't even run away and hide there. She needed to make this conversation last, and have it be better than talking about school.

"So, I have to tell you something," Samus started.

"You do?"

"Uh-huh." Samus's face seemed pained, but also determined to move forward. "I've been thinking about it a lot, and maybe that's why this so awkward right now."

"Awkward?" Jackie laughed. "Whatever do you mean?"

Samus narrowed her eyes then smiled. *Oh, that smile*. Jackie's belly flipped just looking at it.

"So, I remember you from my English class ages ago. I had to look you up again—hence how got your email, since I keep really good records. That's awkward enough as it is, but I also realized I was a huge dick to you when you were in my class."

"You were?"

"Oh yeah. You asked for an extension near the end of the term, and I just went off in an email to you. I was really rude and callous, mostly because I was going through my own shit at the time."

"Really?" Jackie strained her memory. She really didn't like to think about first year, mostly because *everything* had been fucked up then. Her mother had found out she was gay, then found out who she had been dating, and well, that was a long story that she often repressed. But what else had gone on during that year? All Jackie could remember of her English class was thinking it was too easy, so she always left it to the last minute, and then almost failing because she was a fuck up.

"I honestly don't remember," Jackie finally confessed. "What did you say?"

"Just stuff. I don't know. Honestly, I'm relived you don't remember, but I still wanted to apologize."

"No, no, don't worry. I probably deserved it, truthfully."

"What do you mean?"

Jackie took a drink instead of responding. The alcohol warmed her skin and gave her a small confidence boost. "I was just dealing with a lot that year, so it's not surprising that I was fucking around and you probably said something I needed to hear."

"I don't think so. Either way, this is me apologizing. I hate to think I made you terrified to take another English class."

"No offense, but you probably didn't. Really. Don't read too much into things," Jackie realized she was probably being a little short, but Samus seemed to appreciate it. Her eyes lit up for a second then she laughed.

"You're totally right, actually. Let me tell you what I really wanted to say instead of cloaking it in teaching terms." Samus took a deep breath before moving on. "I was actually transitioning during that time period and dealing with a bunch of shit from the admin in the department, not to mention the government and doctors. So I was really cranky all the time to my students—not just you. I apologize for that behaviour, because regardless of what either one of us were going through, I was still in an authority position and shouldn't have been so mean. But, now that I'm no longer in that authority position, I also want you to know now that I'm transgender."

"Oh?" Jackie furrowed her brows. There was a lot of information, delivered in rapid succession, and she still had to parse out what exactly Samus meant. Jackie knew the word transgender, she was pretty sure, but she hadn't really met anyone before. That she knew of, anyway. And if Samus hadn't told her just now, she probably wouldn't have thought she was trans. "I'm sorry to hear that. Not that you were transitioning—or that you're trans—only that it was hard. That admin made it hard."

"It's a lot easier now. I'm done most of the admin stuff now. My name is legally Samus and my markers on everything but my out-of-date Blood Donor card is changed to an F. So that's great. Especially since Ontario changed the law."

"What law?"

Samus smiled awkwardly. "Just a really

outdated law that stated that you absolutely had to have surgery and like seven letters from doctors in order to get anything changed officially. I could tell you more, but any of this info is probably ridiculous and probably boring if you're not trans."

"Not boring, no." Jackie shook her head. "I just don't know anything about it. So I'll probably ask a lot of questions. That can be boring to answer. So..."

When Jackie's gaze met Samus, they both laughed. The awkward silence from before was a lot better. Was it really just because Samus was trans that she was so worried? Man, that was the least of the issues Jackie thought Samus would have. Jackie inched closer to Samus at the bar.

"Can I ask you a question?"

"Yeah, shoot. So long as it's not one of the trifecta questions, I'm okay to answer it."

"Oh no, it sounds like I'm being tested."

"No, no," Samus stated, her face genuine. "There are just a *lot* of questions trans people get asked and I refuse to be an FAQ page for anyone anymore."

"Okay. Can I dare ask what the trifecta questions are?"

"Well, in order, they are: have you had The Surgery, what's your real name, and how do you have sex?"

"Yikes. I wouldn't ask any of those." Jackie paused. "But I was going to ask about your name. This name though."

"Samus?"

"Yeah. Isn't Samus from...." Jackie's eyes

The Big Reveal

trailed to Samus's shirt, and sudden realization dawned on her. "Oh of course. That *is* Samus from *Metroid*."

"I thought you said you'd never played?"

"I don't! But I watch enough video game reviews to know some stuff. Just took me way too long to put everything together. I'm pretty sure I watched a play-through of *The Other M* ages ago, but I forget most of it now, including the name of everyone involved. Maybe I should watch it again before I play it. After the 1986 version, of course."

Samus made a face and launched into a subsequent review-rant about that *Metroid* game. She categorized her criticism like a pro, focusing on play-ability and character development, along with dialogue writing. "Sorry," she mumbled after a few moments. "I've been in academic mode all day and don't know how to shut it off."

"It's okay. I'm learning. You should do YouTube Reviews."

"Maybe." Samus grinned. "This is great, actually. I'm so glad you looked it up. *Metroid* is seriously my vetting process for cool people."

"Really? If they guess where your name is from, they win?"

Samus laughed, her eyes scrunching up as she did. "A little bit, yeah! It's how Lindsey and I met, and we've been super close every since."

"That's amazing. I wish I could do the same thing with my name. Instead I'm endlessly correcting people from Jacqueline to Jackie. I hate Jacqueline. Makes me sound like I'm ninety-five."

"You could change it, you know. Just to Jackie.

I had a friend who was actually born as just Billy, since his parents wanted to cut to the chase."

"Oh, wow. I could, I suppose. But... that's difficult." Jackie slumped in her seat. She couldn't even imagine what her mother would say.

"I get it," Samus said right away. "It's really hard to change your name. The first month of my transition, I accidentally told at least three people my old name—even while I was wearing a dress. Then I signed my emails with my old name because it had been so engrained into me. That was a fun thing to explain to my colleagues. But it passes. You get used to it. And you realize you become much happier, especially if it's the name you know yourself as more."

"I suppose. But it's still difficult."

"Yeah, I get that too. For the people around you, right? Anytime I go home, I have to brace myself for hours before I walk in the door."

"Oh, jeez. I'm so sorry. I can't imagine."

"But you can, in a way," Samus pointed out. "With your own name."

"I suppose so." Jackie's cheeks were red; she knew they were. So she tried to change the topic to not think about her mother anymore. "Huh. I'm still floored by your review of *The Other M*. Is that really all you wrote about today?"

"Sort of. But thank you for the compliment and topic change. I'd totally rather focus on video games than the pitfalls of being trans, especially dating while trans." Samus went to laugh, but instead covered a hand over her mouth. "That is, if we are on a date? Can I safely assume so?"

Jackie's stomach flipped again. The sensation was the same as it was before, she realized, even with what Samus just disclosed. If anything, she liked Samus more now because she was chatty and excited again. Confidence and assured.

"You know," Jackie said. "That was going to be my second question. If this was a date or not. So whatever you want to answer, I'm good with."

Samus grinned. "Then sure, it's a date. Now let me buy you another drink."

~~*

"I would invite you up," Jackie stated. "But about two hours ago, I definitely saw Alicia go up to our room with a woman. I haven't seen her come down since, and I have no texts, so I have a feeling there will be a ray gun outside out door to mark what's going on."

"A ray gun?"

"Oh yeah. We made a bunch of ray guns for our *Hack the Planet* cosplay. Since they're used to take down the secret police, she figured they would be a good way to communicate that there are secret things happening on the other side of the door. Or something. Either way, Alicia is getting lucky right now."

"This sounds like an interesting game."

"We will play, I assure you," Jackie said. "When is the week you want your class to see it?"

"Oh." Samus pulled out her phone, scrolling through a nearly entirely booked up calendar. Jackie sighed a little, and Samus rolled her eyes.

"Oh, I know. Welcome to grad school. Most of these deadlines aren't that serious, but if I don't write them down, I will forget."

"I get it. Mine would be like that, except I don't write anything but raids down."

Samus chuckled. "Okay, so that class is in three weeks. We have plenty of time to figure out the game together first."

"I like the sound of that. Have you ever heard of Snakes and Lattes? It's this board game cafe down on Hunter street."

Samus's eyes widened. "How did I not know about that? I've been in Waterloo for years."

"I have my secret hideaways in the city."

"Oh? Sounds like there's a story there. I would love to hear more about that."

Jackie grinned. "It helps when one of your friends is an architect. He has the entire city mapped out for good larping and photo shoot places. I could show you around sometime, too."

"Let's not get too ahead of ourselves, or I won't be able to put it in my calendar."

"Sorry, sorry, I get excited really easily."

"Hey, that's great. Don't apologize for that at all." Samus placed her hand over Jackie's on the bar. Their eyes lingered for a moment as Jackie's heart rate rose. *Are we going to kiss?* Before she could decide if that was too soon or just right, Samus glanced down at her phone. She read out the date and time for Jackie, but she barely heard. She stared at Samus's chin and cheeks. *Will she be soft? Or rough?* Jackie trembled slightly, wanting to find out.

"That time sound good to you?"

"Yeah," Jackie said. "It's great."

"Good. Because I would also like to invite you back to my room, but Lindsey has requested that we have an early bedtime so we can drive back tomorrow and beat the traffic."

"Right, right. We'll get our timing down eventually." When Jackie glanced down at her phone, she was surprised to see it was nearly midnight. The bar had gotten more crowded as they talked, but now it was only late night party goers who nursed their drinks. "I think I should head back."

"You gonna be okay if you can't get into your room?"

"Oh yeah. There are lots of people here I know. I'll be fine. I'm probably going to try and text a few of them before I head up, though."

"Okay, sounds good." Samus tucked in her stool as she got up then waited for Jackie. When Samus held her arms out, there was a silent question on her face. Jackie stepped into the hug right away, wrapping her arms around Samus. The gesture was small, but the contact between their bodies excited her. Her mind was still bubbling up with questions and plans for each other, but she knew they would have time now.

"Goodnight," Samus said.

"Goodnight."

With a small wave, Samus headed to the elevator. As soon as she disappeared, Jackie sat back down at the bar and started to Google.

When Alicia texted her thirty minutes later,

Jackie was halfway through an article on transgender identity on college campuses. *Yo yo yo*, the message from Alicia stated. *how are you? sorry I stole the room.*

It's cool. I definitely just had a date so I spent my time wisely.

!!!! Alicia wrote back. *where are you? imma come and get you oh my god tell me everything.*

I'm in the bar down here. Don't worry, there's not much to tell. Except that I used to be her student.

i'm in love already. may/december????

Jackie thought for a moment. She had just turned twenty-five earlier in the month. Samus couldn't have been more than thirty, so five years, at most, probably wasn't enough to fulfil the May/December requirements.

No, not really. But she's really nerdy. Jackie waited, wondering if she needed to add, 'and she's trans'. For the past half hour, Jackie had read article after article about how transgender people didn't want to reduce their identity to that and only that. So Jackie held off telling Alicia, at least, for now. *And I think I'm seeing her next week. She's actually in this hotel and...*

Alicia wrote her back before she could even finish the message. *kk, i just kicked michelle out and have ordered room service for us. now come back up here and be my duo and tell me all about her. okay? then I can tell you about a weird thing michelle can do with her tongue that i'm determined to pass on to as many people as possible.*

Sure. Be right there. Jackie laughed. *Would that tongue trick even be useful for me?* Jackie wondered, then shook her head. *Don't get too far ahead. Just one step at a time.* For once, Jackie was patient enough to wait.

Chapter Seven

Jackie balled fists at her side and tried not to scream. Her mother hovered just outside the dressing room door. Her shoes tapped against the floor; each sound felt as if it pounded into Jackie's brain. *This isn't real, this isn't real, this isn't real,* Jackie chanted to herself. When she opened her eyes, she sighed. In the dressing room mirror, she barely recognized herself.

The orange hair was gone, dyed black as soon as the con was over. The short hair remained, Alicia giving a couple more trims to frame Jackie's face better and so it was less Julian Howard and more Jackie.

Now, though, it felt as if Alicia's hard work had been undone. Jackie stood in a floor length dress with skinny straps over her shoulders. Her sports bra was visible underneath the dress, making everything look completely ridiculous. Jackie knew the first words her mother would say when she stepped out of the dressing room would be 'take off your bra' or 'we need to get you a new bra', but Jackie wasn't going to have it. *You don't understand,* she thought, *I need to keep this on.*

"Jacqueline?" her mother called. "Is everything okay?"

"No..." Jackie murmured. Ever since picking up

the car from her mother, Jackie knew she'd have to pay for it in some way. Not with money, but with her time, and apparently, her sense of self too. When her mother called her the Wednesday after returning it, Jackie avoided picking up. But when talking to Samus, Jackie let her guard down, and she accidentally answered a call from her mother a few days ago. That's when grad dress shopping had been suggested, and Jackie knew there was no way to get out of it, short of setting the store on fire.

And really, setting the store on fire right now looked to be a good idea. Except that with her luck, her mother would somehow manage to save this hideous dress, and Jackie would be back at square one.

"Just a minute," Jackie said. "I'm trying to figure out how to do the zipper up."

"I can help. Let me in. I want to see how beautiful you are."

Jackie wanted to vomit. She knew everything her mother said was with the best of intentions, but it still made her skin crawl. She undid the dress zipper, and begrudgingly took off her bra and added it to her pile of clothing. The dress had some kind of built in bra for Jackie's small chest, so she could wear the dress with nothing underneath. Even with the dress over her arms again, she still felt naked. Her boobs were... just *too* big. And they weren't even that big at all.

"Jacqueline, please."

"Jackie, mom. Call me Jackie."

"Jackie, then. May I come in?"

A stern tone. Jackie knew she couldn't avoid this any longer. Without another word, she tapped the lock on the dressing room door. Right away, her mother swooped inside and swooned.

"Oh, the colour! Purple goes so well with your skin and eyes."

"Thanks."

"You don't like it?"

Jackie shrugged. "Doesn't seem to matter what I like."

"Jackie." Her mother's eyes narrowed. She folded her arms across her chest, cinching her power suit at the side. "You know we want what's best for you."

"You and Jim? Yeah, I know. I just don't understand why we need graduation photos with a dress. I thought that's what the cap and gown were for? Nice and neutral, everyone's the same. You know, like prison uniforms."

"That's exactly why I don't want photos wearing those. You need to dress for success now that you have a degree."

"And mountains of student debt. I mean, where is this success you speak of? It's not like I have a job offer lined up." Jackie knew she must be getting desperate to be out of this situation when she brought up money and her future. That was a big black hole she never wanted to touch—especially around her mom.

"I know things are hard. The economy isn't the best, but that's why you have a math degree. You know the numbers when people are too afraid to know them, right?" Her mother didn't wait for

The Big Reveal

Jackie to response. "Have you applied any places?"

"A couple." She had applied to two earlier that week, so that was plural, and she wasn't lying. One job application was to a fabric store and the other was to a bank, so it kind of evened out.

"Then you should start thinking positively. Change your thoughts, change your life. And suddenly, the world will open to you."

Jackie made a face in the mirror that her mother didn't see. She had been spewing the same kind of New Age-y nonsense for the last four years, ever since she met Jim, Jackie's step-father. The two of them were 'magically pulled together' through her 'good thoughts into the world.' Now Delia had a new job, new house, and a new outlook on life.

And if only Jackie would open up to it, then her life would be oh so different too! Jackie wanted to retch anytime she thought of her mom's life coaching business cards or the esoteric slogans that hung above her home office.

"You know me," Jackie finally said. "I'd much rather play pretend than change my thoughts."

"I know. You and your games and your costumes. That's fun, but you should really put your efforts towards the future."

"Pretending is the future, though." Jackie paused for a moment, trying to think of something Samus had said to her late at night this week when she was lesson planning. Though there was no way for Jackie to get into her course—demand was so high, and she had to finish up her math degree anyway—she was constantly kept in the loop so she felt as if she really was attending twice a week. "Pretending is like imagining, and if you can imagine a future, then you can make it real. You know? That's why sci-fi is really important, and why a lot of technology that was on *Star Trek* ended up being invented. We needed to see it to know we could do it."

"Huh. Interesting perspective. Have you been taking some philosophy classes along with your degree?"

"Not really. Just talking about books a lot with this woman I know."

"Well," her mother sad, clearly catching the tone of the relationship. "I'm happy for you and this woman. I'd like to meet her soon. But I still think that pretending, while important, can only be reasonable if that future is an option. No point pretending with dinosaurs when they're all extinct, right?"

"You never know. I could make the next Jurassic Park."

"Please. My patience, dear. Let me take a photo of you in the dress for Jim to see his opinion."

"Really? Jim?"

"What? He used to paint houses, and now he builds them. He's got a good eye for design and fashion."

Jackie sighed. She didn't fight with her mother though, knowing full-well this was a losing battle. Even if she resented the way her mother was almost so blindingly positive the past few years, Jackie knew this was far better than her having a fit each time she mentioned a girl she was dating. It had taken a long, long time to get to this point, and though Delia was a nightmare sometimes, at least it was the kind of nightmare that ended up with Jackie in a purple dress and not homeless on the street.

"There," her mother said. She lowered the phone and began to text. "Thank you for that. I think you look beautiful."

"I think you look like a tool," she murmured to her reflection. When she heard her phone buzz from the bench where her jeans were, she shuffled over, nearly falling in the process.

"Careful now," her mother said, catching her arm. "Maybe we need to get you some shoes to go with this. Heels, so the dress won't be too long and trail on the ground."

"Oh please. No. I want flats."

"We'll think about it. Right now, I want to get this for sure and, if needed, we can hem."

"Okay. Thanks, I guess..." Jackie grabbed the price tag and flipped it over. Her eyes nearly bugged out of her head. "I can't get this."

"Why not?"

"It's so expensive! I could make something better."

"Well, why don't you?"

"Really?" For a moment, the suits and ties Jackie had been brainstorming the past two weeks came to her mind. There was only a second of excitement before she realized her mother wasn't suggesting Jackie make a suit, but knock off version of the dress.

"Hmm, you know, this might work. We can take some more photos to get the pattern down and I'll get you the fabric, and voila. Would that be better, do you think? Would you wear the dress if you got to make it?"

Jackie drew quiet. It somehow seemed worse, to make a dress she knew she'd be uncomfortable with than to just allow whatever fashion designer this was. "Does it have to be purple?"

"Well, I like it. I think you look good in it. But I suppose... "

"Okay," Jackie said. "I'll make it. So long as it's not purple."

Her mother clapped her hands together. "Excellent! In this case, it could be a fun little project. Now, let me take some more pictures, and we'll see if we can't create something good, yes?"

Though Jackie's phone went off again, she ignored it and allowed her mother to take a few more pictures and write down some numbers. Then Delia headed towards the dressing room doors.

"I'll be just outside in the parking lot," she said. "Finish up in here and come find me so I can drop you off for your little study date."

Jackie didn't even care that her mother was teasing her now about the date she clearly had with Samus after this. Jackie stripped off the dress in a massive hurry and shimmed her jeans back on. Her bra felt tight, but *so* much better over her chest again. When she pulled out her phone, she read the messages from Samus with a smile.

Gah. My alarm went off a lot later than I

thought. I'm on my way now, but I may be late.

Don't worry about it, Jackie replied. *I'm just on my way now. So really, you're just in time.*

Perfect! See you soon. Samus followed the message with a small heart emoji. It wasn't much, but Jackie already felt so much better.

Chapter Eight

Samus was *definitely* late.

Since she warned Jackie right away, she didn't have to worry that it looked as if she was standing her up on their second official date. Since the conference, they kept up a steady dialogue through text messages and even fell into a routine of talking between ten-thirty to one in the morning. That was usually the time of night when Samus decided she had done enough work for the day, had dinner, and was about to relax with Netflix. For Jackie, it seemed like eleven or so at night was when she was about to start sewing. She had started to rack up several commission jobs from other cosplayers in the anime community and seemed to be doing quite well. She had even applied for a job at the fabric store to get a discount and sometimes, when she was tired enough, talked to Samus about starting her own business.

Since I'm good with numbers, obviously, Jackie wrote. *And apparently I should start to think good thoughts and my future will open up to me.*

Most conversations between them were light and fun. But Samus still couldn't tell how much they were allowed to ask one another or how personal they could get. She hoped that after this semi-formal date in the afternoon at a games cafe, that boundary would be a lot easier to cross.

Samus grabbed a cup of coffee from the front counter, along with a brownie, before she slid into one of the side booths near the door. One wall of Snakes and Lattes was lined with side to side shelves absolutely filled with board games. She spotted the typical classics like *Monopoly*, *Clue*, and *Candyland,* followed by more obscure games like *Carcassonne*, *Munchkins*, and the classic *Super Exploring Dungeon*.

No way! This is awesome, Samus thought. Leaving her coffee and brownie aside, she nabbed the brightly coloured *Super Exploring Dungeon* for her booth. She had watched the Kickstarter when it was first launched, but was unable to participate since all her money at the time was going towards hormone therapy. She had watched YouTube videos of the game, though, and knew it was right up her alley since it was a board game designed to mimic an NES video game. She took off the lid and sorted through the pieces, feeling like she was twelve again and playing *Metroid* for the first time.

After ten minutes of wallowing in nostalgia with the game, Samus was still alone. *Odd.* When she glanced at her phone, she saw no new messages from Jackie. She put the game aside from now, grabbing her coffee and her course marking, and hoped this task would make the time go faster. By the time Jackie did show up, almost thirty minutes had passed and Samus had already graded over half of her classes' first assignment.

"I'm *so* sorry." Jackie made her way right to Samus's table, her face red and apologetic. "I pretty much had to run here."

"What? Why?"

"My mom dropped me off around the corner. I didn't want her to actually see where I was going. So I ran after I made sure she wasn't close by. Which is odd, I know. I'm sorry I'm late. She just talks *so* much sometimes, and I hate explaining stuff to her."

Samus flinched. She tried to brush off the sudden sting, wondering if Jackie was ashamed of her or not. *Probably not. Don't always think the worst.* "It's okay," Samus said instead. "I'm one to talk for being late. And besides, I got some time to grade."

"Oh, wow!" Jackie eyed the stack of papers then the games. "You've been busy."

"I haven't played anything yet. But I wanted to grab the good ones before they were taken."

Jackie surveyed the area. There were only a couple other people there, intensely playing chess or organizing a small table full of Cards Against Humanity. "Well, thank you. Let me go get some food and then we can start with *Hack the Planet*. Or do you want to start with *Super Exploring Dungeon?* I've never played it before, but I followed the Kickstarter. I had no money at the time so I couldn't get in. Did you follow it?"

Samus grinned. Oh, she was so silly to doubt Jackie. "I did, actually. All the pieces for *Super Exploring Dungeon* are already out, so if you want to start here, then I'm definitely in. We can get to

Hack the Planet afterwards, if you want. I'm not in any rush."

"Great. Neither am I."

~~*

After a couple cups of coffee, they were halfway through a *Super Exploring Dungeon* round with Samus acting as the board master. "What do you think so far?"

"This is much longer than I thought it'd be," Jackie said with a laugh. "But I like it. A lot of fun."

"It reminds me of playing 8-bit games as a kid. Totally nostalgic for my brother and I on Saturday morning, you know?" When Samus rolled and Jackie didn't really say anything else, Samus asked, "Do you have any siblings?"

"I do. But we all live pretty far from one another now and my mother's remarried. So I see my step-siblings more."

Samus nodded. She completed her turn then drank a few sips of coffee while Jackie did her turn. "Do you mind if I ask something?"

Jackie laughed. "I think we're both doing that a lot."

"Fair enough. I always like to tread lightly before personal issues. I suppose I'm very aware of boundaries."

As soon as Samus said that, Jackie crashed through one of the walls on the board. They laughed and chatted about the game dynamics for a moment, before Jackie finally nodded. "Ask away. If it's really difficult to say aloud, then I'll just text you the answer."

Samus chuckled. "Good deal. So... what was the personal thing you had going on during English 101 the first time?"

Jackie's face faltered. Samus thought she was about to actually grab her phone and text the response, instead. "You really don't have to tell me. I can understand wanting to leave some issues behind."

"No, no, it's fine. It's nothing something that's in the past, really. It's just... Okay, so I'm gay, right?"

"I hope so," Samus said. "Or at least, I hope you like women."

"Totally. But in first year, I hadn't told my mom yet. I knew when I was in high school. Alicia, my best friend, is also bi and we kind of dated, but it didn't work out. Our personalities aren't the kind that go together like that, though I've lived with her for almost five years now, and I think we'd probably get married if we're still single at forty. So I already knew I was gay, but I never told my mom. I figured why bother? She has things she believes, and I don't have to crush her fantasy."

"I get that," Samus said. "I really do. But don't let me cut you off."

"No, that's actually a relief to hear you understand. So many people are always like 'the truth will set you free'; they expect you to come out at a moment's notice because you're lying if you're not. I never felt that way. Why should I tell people every last intimate detail? So I never did, unless I was fucking them." Jackie laughed a bit, and Samus noted the way she went to curl hair around her ear, but couldn't complete the nervous tick because her hair was now short.

"It's kind of the same with trans stuff," Samus added. "When disclosing could get me fired or worse, I tend to not tell anyone. Intimate situations are different. I identify as bisexual, mostly preferring women, but I'm usually chased out of lesbian spaces. So I always feel as if I have to disclose before I go on a date with someone. Some people are cool, and others are not. It's a gamble every time."

"I'm cool. Right?"

"Indeed! Totally cool. But seriously, I'm going to stop talking soon to let you finish. Because I'm assuming you're not done? Something must have changed your mind about coming out to your mom."

"Not changed, really. I still think coming out is bullshit, but I was persuaded. I um, I started to date my professor that semester. Things got really heated really quickly. I spent all my time with her, and I was just so far gone. She was tenured, forty-something, and one of the best names in her field. I think she felt untouchable—who doesn't when you have tenure?—and so she wanted to show me off. Talked about me all the time. I ended up dropping her course so we could keep dating, and that was a bad move because it was the only one I was passing."

You passed mine, Samus wanted to add, but knew she had interrupted too much already. She folded her hands, intently focused on Jackie as she tried to work through the rest of her story.

"I got a call from my mom asking about my grades, and well, I came out. I told her I was gay, and in love with someone. She was shocked and angry, but only because I was failing. She wasn't really that upset about the gay thing. Then I brought home Maureen, and my mom flipped out because Maureen was a prof."

"That sucks," Samus said when Jackie had paused for a while. "I'm really sorry."

"It's really not as bad as I think it is. That's what Alicia always says. My mom was never actually upset at me for being gay. She was mad I was a failure and brought home someone twice my age. But not because I was gay. I think I wanted her to be mad at me being gay, so I could be without fault, you know? If she didn't like me because I was gay, then it was her problem and not mine."

"Hey." Samus reached out to touch Jackie's hand. "You can still be upset. There's clearly something from your mom you're not getting. Even if you can't find words for what's missing, something is. And sometimes that's enough."

"Yeah, I guess so. It's really frustrating not having words, though. I want to be mad, but then I box myself into a corner because I can't find a reason why and I look like a petulant child. Like today, when I was talking with her. I was so upset she wanted to buy me a dress. She was offering to pay, said I looked beautiful, and yet, I wanted to scream."

"Really? What do you need the dress for, if I

can ask?"

"Oh, I'm graduating soon. So we were shopping for graduation dresses because she wants a photo of me in something other than my cap and gown. I don't know why I just can't wear my Julian Howard suit, but hey, if mommy wants it, then I get it."

"You should have some say, though. You're the one wearing it!" Samus paused for a moment, debating whether or not to share her own story. When Jackie remained quiet, Samus went on. "You know, when I started to see a lot of doctors during my transition, many of them asked why I wasn't in a dress."

"Really?"

"Yeah. In their heads, if I was really a woman, then wouldn't I want to wear a dress all the time? Especially if I hadn't been allowed to up until then. But I walked in with jeans and a T-shirt, and they were confused, because 'guys can wear this, so how are you different?' It's not the point whether or not guys can wear something. It was never the clothing that made me upset."

"What was it then?"

"How people saw me in that clothing. I didn't want people to think I was a sissy guy. I hated that. But it took me forever to realize that it wasn't me being afraid of all things feminine that made me hate being called a sissy. I wanted to be a masculine—or vaguely butch—woman. When I started to think of myself that way, *everything* changed. I knew I didn't want to wear a dress, but I wanted to see an F on my license."

"Huh." Jackie was quiet for some time. Her gaze flitted over the game in front of them, halfway through the dungeon underground. Though it was her roll, she didn't pick up the dice.

"Have I said too much?" Samus asked. "I do that sometimes. And some people are really unsure of what being trans actually means, so I can often confuse them even more because I'm not like Caitlyn Jenner. Not in the least."

"No, no. You haven't confused me. I liked that story, actually. Don't think that being trans bugs me. It really doesn't."

Good, Samus thought, *because then we can kiss.* She wanted to shove all the game pieces to the floor in that instant and kiss Jackie where she sat. Seeing her so torn up over a dress resonated so much, and Samus wanted to swoop her into her arms and comfort her baby butch soul. *I don't even know how she identifies, really. Maybe she doesn't want to be butch, and she just hates dresses. Who knows?*

"Anyway," Jackie said, running her hands through her hair. "I think I may have struck a bargain with my mom because I'm going to make the dress now."

"Are you?"

"Oh yeah. I'm still kind of bummed—because I don't like dresses, and now I have to make my own demise—but maybe if I keep what you said in mind about how I look in the dress that matters, the clothing won't as much. Thanks."

Before anything else could be said, Jackie

rolled the dice. It made her small paladin move two steps forward. This triggered a boss fight, and soon they lost themselves in the game. Since Jackie was playing three heroes and Samus all the villains, their back and forth battle went on for a while. When Samus looked up, she realized there was no sun in the sky.

"Oh man," Samus said. "How late is it?"

"Oh. Shit. It's almost eight. How long has this game been going?"

"Over three hours! Wow." Samus let out a breath. "I don't think I've played one this long. The cafe closes in an hour or so, too."

"Should we finish this or go onto *Hack the Planet*?"

"I think I want to finish this since we're so close. Either one of us could win."

"Yeah, I think you're right. Sorry *Hack the Planet*." Jackie laughed as she put the card deck back into her bag. "We kinda suck for totally forgetting about it."

"But we'll get there," Samus said. "I know we will. That is, if you want to see me again?"

"Yeah," Jackie said. "I think I do. Now roll. I'm about to destroy your dragon and take the kingdom for myself."

"We'll see, paladin. We'll see."

~~*

Jackie won. By the end of the game, there was only her paladin and one dragon on the board. It came down to three dice rolls, and only one point won the entire match. Jackie let out an exalted cry over her victory just as the waitress came over and slipped them their bill. They paid at the front, each for their own meals, and then walked towards the door.

"Will you be running home?" Samus asked. "Or taking the bus?"

"Walking probably. I'm really close by." Jackie shuddered a little under her large coat. Samus noticed her neck was bare now because of her new haircut, and instinctively went to unwrap her green scarf.

"Here, take this. You'll need it if you're walking."

"Are you sure—"

"Yes. I'm taking the bus, and it'll come in a little bit. You need to keep warm." Samus stepped forward, looping the scarf around Jackie's neck then tucking it in front of her. Their hands brushed and their eyes met again.

This is it, Samus thought. *Finally.* As soon as their mouths met, Jackie made a small noise. Somewhat in shock, maybe, or in pleasure. Samus couldn't be sure. She moved against Jackie, her lips parting a little as she pressed firmly. When their noses brushed, and Samus felt how cold Jackie was, she broke the kiss to pull her tightly into a hug.

"You sure you don't want to get warm somewhere first? I'm concerned about your nose."

"It's always like this," Jackie said. "I'm always freezing."

"I hear you. That's mostly estrogen's fault, actually. I never used to have cold hands until I started taking it."

"Really?" Jackie asked, genuinely shocked. "I never considered that before. But it makes so much sense."

"Indeed. And since we both have no testosterone to keep us warm, we obviously need each other." Samus squeezed Jackie again, keeping their bodies close. Her line before was a bit cheesy, she had to admit, but Samus was relieved when Jackie also smiled along.

"Sure. You know. I wish I had more time."

"I wish you did too. Text me later and we'll figure out something else, okay?"

"Sure." Jackie initiated the kiss this time. Her fingers reached out and along Samus's jaw line, then up to her hair. Samus didn't feel like she normally did when people touched her cheeks— on edge, worried about the abrasive stubble of what she hadn't gotten rid of yet through electrolysis. But this was easier, better. Jackie wasn't feeling for the edges of a man hidden under a woman's skin; she was looking for Samus, touching her, and keeping her warm.

"Thank you," Jackie said when she pulled away from the kiss. "I had fun today."

"Yeah, me too."

With another wave, and a lingering smile, Jackie headed up Hunter Street, towards one of the old art museums that was now an archive. Samus went to the bus stop, her smile never leaving her face.

Chapter Nine

Jackie closed the door then turned around to place her back against it. She breathed a heavy sigh. She tried to convince herself it was only the winter chill that made her move so slowly and tremble where she stood. But there was also Samus. The way her surprisingly soft body felt in Jackie's arm made Jackie want to sweep her away. *She's so much shorter than me,* Jackie thought. *I wonder if I really could pick her up and carry her away?*

Jackie shook off the thought before toeing off her winter shoes and discarding her jacket. She could already smell the incense Alicia was burning, and wasn't surprised to find her hunched over the kitchen table, a deck of tarot cards next to her and some kind of freshly baked cookie cooling on the stove.

"Hey, hey." Alicia barely looked up from her cards. "How was your date?"

"Good. Can I eat one of these?"

"Sure. Go for it. It's for the New Moon. You know we're gonna have a blue moon in a couple weeks? I'm so excited."

"I can imagine." Jackie bit into the cookie, tasting overpowering vanilla and sugar. "I should probably make a real dinner soon, but this will sustain me until then."

"You didn't eat with her? You were out so long, I just figured you two got dinner. Oh... were you?" Alicia grinned extra wide. She finally peeled her eyes away from the tarot cards but left the spread as it was. "Did you two get more familiar with one another?"

"Not in the way you're thinking. We were actually playing a game for like, four hours straight."

"Wow. Impressive. Was it the *Hack the Planet*? I didn't think games could go that long."

"No, actually! We were into *Super Exploring Dungeon*. You remember that one, right?" When Alicia nodded, Jackie went on. "Well, it was fun. We just kind of suck with the whole *Hack the Planet* thing. But we'll eventually play it." Jackie laughed a little as she brought out a pot for boiling water. Pasta, like always, was the easiest choice in her kitchen.

"Huh. I guess. But wasn't that the entire reason you two were getting together? What about her class?"

"Oh. Right. Samus probably has something else set up."

"All right. But why are you avoiding *Hack the Planet*? If you're playing *Super Exploring Dungeon*, you're clearly still into showing her your nerd side."

"She met me in full cosplay at the con. I think I'm beyond hiding the nerdiness."

"Then what's keeping you two from playing?"

"Don't know." Jackie shrugged.

As she ran water from the tap into the pot, Jackie went through the *Hack the Planet* deck in her mind. In the same way Alicia sometimes used the tarot cards to help her make a decision, or to just check in and see how she felt, Jackie sometimes used the game cards. She knew it was stupid; *Hack the Planet* was a cyberpunk game made by a corporation, not even a pseudo-form of divination. Ever since she dressed up as Julian Howard, though, the cards pulled her in even further. She no longer wanted to be the villain in the neon suit, so she had started to brainstorm some ideas for an OC. Maybe, if she created a super-awesome male hacker for the game, she could make her own cards and add them to the deck—or even better, pitch the idea to the people who made the game.

Jackie nodded to herself. Maybe this explained why she wasn't showing Hack the Planet to Samus; in her mind, the game wouldn't be finished until her OC was part of the deck.

"Anyway," Alicia said, "I suppose it's just a game, so it doesn't really matter. It's all about foreplay until you get to the fun parts. So... Are you excited about those fun parts?"

Jackie chuckled before her cheeks went red. Alicia squealed and kicked out a chair across from her.

"Come sit. We must talk," Alicia said.

Jackie groaned. "Why? You should talk first. Why are you asking the cards about your fate tonight? Is it to do with Michelle?"

"Well, I did get The Lovers card. But that's

more about a decision than it is about actual lovers."

"So is that a yes? Are you and Michelle serious enough to worry about the future with?"

"Maybe. I really like her, we have fun, but I think it's a fling. Right now I think I need to decide whether or not I should stay at my job or venture out into something more. Like owning my own business."

"Oh." Jackie was taken aback as she sat down. "You've never struck me as the entrepreneur type."

"I didn't think so. But I pulled a lot of pentacles in this round, and that's the money suit, and maybe I should be more open to the idea. Who knows? That's a conversation for another day, and you, math genius, may be able to help there." Alicia grinned as she shuffled her spread away into the deck again. "But right now, tell me about Samus."

"What is there to know, really? I told you everything." Jackie's gaze wandered over to the pot, though there was no way it had boiled over in such a short amount of time.

A few nights after they got back from the con, Jackie had explained to Alicia that Samus was trans. Over a text message, Samus had said it was okay to tell people she was (since most people know anyway), but Jackie was still shaky on the proper terminology. She had spent an entire weekend reading *Whipping Girl* on a recommendation from Samus, and when Alicia had found the book, it allowed for an easy conversation to develop about it.

"Yeah, sure," Alicia said. "You told me she's trans, and on hormones, and that her boobs are bigger than yours. But how do you feel about her? Have you even kissed yet?"

"Yeah. We have. Tonight, actually."

"And?"

"And? It was cold."

"Cold? What's that supposed to mean?"

"It's winter in Canada. We kissed, but I barely felt her lips."

"Well, that's a lie." Alicia huffed. When the water boiled on the stove, Alicia was the one who got up to put the pasta in while Jackie stayed put. As she stirred the water, Alicia curled her hair behind her ear, asking coyly, "Are you nervous?"

"For what? Sex. I've had sex before. A lot, actually."

"I know. But even then you were nervous. Are you... you know. What is the right way to ask about Samus and her... you know?"

"As far as I've read, there's no right way to ask about any trans person's genitals. That's private, or something."

"Hmm. That's difficult. Because all relationships need to talk about sex. You should ask her."

"About what's in her pants? That's... awkward."

"Well, if you're hoping to put your mouth on it in some way, then you need to be mature enough to ask about it."

Jackie laughed. So much tension had been

building up at this issue in her mind and she didn't even realize it until that moment. She was nervous, scared, and completely unsure of what to do. She didn't want to be rude or feel as if she was policing Samus's identity. Samus was a woman, and there was no way Jackie even thought of her as anything but a woman. But what would sex be like? It was exciting to think about, but she was also in the dark.

"Maybe we should just have sex with the lights off," Jackie said. "And see what we find?"

"Isn't that what a lot of straight people do? I'd never thought I'd see the day... What has happened to my lovely lesbian Jackie?"

"Nothing. I just..."

"Shush, it's fine. You know I'm teasing, right?"

"Yeah, yeah. You're a barrel of laughs." Jackie shrugged. The distinctions of straight and gay were starting to blur a lot in the past few weeks. Same with male and female; masculine and feminine. Jackie didn't realize it, but she had become fixated on the difference between a masculine woman and a feminine man. Which one was Jackie? She hated being seen as the girly girl, but she didn't really like being called butch, either. *Would femme guy work, though?*

"What was that?" Alicia asked. Her brow was furrowed and fixated on Jackie.

"What was what?"

"You smiled for a second there. Did you think of a position that would be super fun? Or a toy? Oh my goddess, I really hope Samus has toys. That could be so much fun for both of you."

"No, I wasn't think about that. I don't think I should, really, right now. I think I should just ask her before any type of fantasies go wild."

"Well, yeah. Duh. But you know I love sharing. If you don't want to, that's cool. But I'm gonna tell you more about Michelle. Can I?" Alicia's green eyes glowed with excitement.

Jackie sighed but smiled. Yeah, she *definitely* wanted to hear about Michelle if it meant she could just stop thinking about gender and sex for a little while longer. "So long as you're going to keep making me pasta, I'm game."

"Excellent." Alicia got the strainer, prepared the sauce, and launched into her story.

"By the way," Alicia added after several hours of gabbing and asking the tarot cards for advice (yielding no real results but a lot more pentacle cards), "your mom stopped by earlier."

Jackie froze. "She did? What did she want?"

"Just to drop off some fabric. She said you two had made a plan earlier? I don't know. I just let her in. I think she dropped the stuff off in your room."

Jackie was still frozen. *Right. The dress.* She would eventually have to do that.

"Have I done something wrong?" Alicia asked. "I could just pretend I'm not home next some she comes."

"No, it's fine. You did the right thing. I just forgot about it. The fabric is for a new project."

"Oh, look at you. Taking *so* many commissions. Maybe we really can start a business together. The cards seem to want it." Alicia winked as she picked up the plates and put them in the sink. It was late now, definitely time to pack it in, as much as Jackie suddenly wanted to talk about this new business idea. With Alicia's acumen for style and Jackie's stubbornness and math stats, they could do something cool. She was sure of it. *And if the cards think so, too...*

But it would all have to happen another night. When Alicia yawned and complained about work for the next day, they said goodnight and went into their separate bedrooms. Jackie, still too wired from so much coffee, looked at the rolls and rolls of purple fabric on her bed.

I thought we decided on no purple? She huffed. *Fine. Maybe I can trim it with black or something.* Jackie sifted through her emails to gather more patterns from her mother and set up her sewing machine. In the far back of the closet, she spotted her Julian Howard suit.

I could do it again, right? A suit for graduation? Not quite a business pantsuit like her mother wore, but a nice suit. *I could do it, right?*

There was only one way to find out.

~~*

Making a suit was much harder than Jackie expected. When it wasn't for cosplay but for "real life," she had to make sure it was perfect by her standards—and everyone else's. The fabric she had was all wrong, too, and her excessive trips back and forth to the fabric store were going to make her go broke. By the time she had finished the suit jacket and patterns for a tie, she realized she was being foolish. *Why am I wasting my time on something like this? Ugh.* Her actual graduation was in the middle of May, which always seemed far away, but definitely wasn't anymore. Her courses were almost all done, and though her grades weren't the best, she was going to pass.

It's all going to be over soon, and instead of feeling free, I just feel trapped. Jackie's mom had been emailing and texting her a lot, asking for updates. She was going to go and buy the dress anyway, her impatience winning. So Jackie would be left with fabric and two half-finished projects, and feel even more like a failure.

"Leesha?" Jackie called out. Jackie had been cooped up in her room so long she lost track of time. It was past seven at night, but there was no sigh of Alicia. When Jackie spotted a note on the fridge door, she squinted to read.

Out. Seeing Michelle. Have your girl over, since I'll be gone all night. Wink, wink.

Jackie sighed. She had been avoiding Samus too. *But, in my defense,* Jackie thought, *so has Samus.* Since the date at the board game cafe, they exchanged a couple "I had so much fun" texts and a couple more complaining about workload, but nothing much. Still nervous, Jackie finally sent a new message.

Hey, Samus. You around? What's going on?

You know how it is, she wrote back moments later. *Grading on a Friday night so I can reward myself with TV later. You?*

Sewing a dress I don't want to wear. The usual.

Oh, that sucks.

Jackie nodded, but didn't want to dwell on that issue anymore. For once, sewing wasn't her happy place, and that fact was killing her. *Do you want to come over? I can help you grade, and you can watch TV here.*

That really does sound amazing, but I can't. I totally forgot just how many assignments I made in this class, and in spite of loving the material, I still suck at grading. I have to give this back to everyone by tonight so they can revise for their bigger project.

Bigger project?

Oh wow! I didn't tell you? I'm getting them to create their own fantasy landscape as an exercise in world-building. I'm even trying to rent out space in an art gallery or some place for them to display it.

That sounds amazing, Jackie wrote and meant every bit of it. Her mind drifted to the OC she was still brainstorming for *Hack the Planet*. *Can they borrow from existing universes? Because I'd know exactly what I'd want to do.*

Yes and no. I have one student using tarot cards as her main fantasy landscape, but she's still tweaking it. So long as their work isn't a straight up retelling, then they're solid. I'm reading their proposals now, actually.

That's sweet. Alicia likes tarot cards, so I know that would be an interesting display.

You should come! Samus wrote a minute later. *You could have a display, too, if you wanted.*

But I'm not in your class.

So? I like you, and you've been in one of my classes before. So what if there's a random person at the showing? I think you'd fit right in, actually.

Jackie smiled at the message. *I like hearing that. Should I let you go, though? Allow you to focus?*

No... I like talking to you. I miss you.

Jackie's stomach flipped again. *I really miss you too. Sorry I've been flakey.*

It's okay. So have I. This only means we need to make a plan, so we can keep seeing one another, right?

Right.

Good. So maybe on Friday afternoon we can hang out? So it's at the start of the weekend, and nothing else can get in our way?

Okay, sure. I think I'd like that a lot.

As she waited for Samus to respond, Jackie brought down the kettle from the cupboard and made herself a cup of tea. The water was boiled by the time a message came through.

Good. You're in my calendar. Do you want to talk tonight, though? So long as you don't mind my long pauses...

No. I don't' mind. In fact, I have a game.

A game?

Okay, less of a game and more of a fandom reference.

Well, now you have my attention. I'm listening.

Jackie grinned at her screen. She typed fast so she didn't lose her nerve. *So, let's play Quid Pro Quo. I'm an FBI investigator and you're a prisoner*

The Big Reveal

I'm extracting information from. Or the other way around. Basically, we're just asking each other random stuff without worrying about the question. Does that make sense?

It does. And I love Hannibal, this is great, Samus replied faster than before. *You first?*

Jackie swallowed. She knew this game was a high concept way of getting Samus to answer the questions that had been on Jackie's mind more than ever. But she started small. *Where is your family from?*

Oh, just outside Ottawa. Small town. Everyone's bilingual, but I never see them anymore, Samus replied, and incidentally answered two of Jackie's questions right away.

Samus followed up with her question: *At the cafe, you told me you hid a lot in the city. Where's your favourite spot?*

The movie theatre. The independent one, just outside downtown. I like it there because it's easy to sneak into since it shares space with a coffee bar. So long as you don't actually sneak into a movie itself, no one cares if you're in the lobby with all the strange statues for hours. I've definitely hidden there, right in plain sight, for an entire evening and no one noticed until closing time. Jackie paused. She had hidden there all evening when she first told her mother about her older girlfriend, and then returned to the statues when Maureen had broken her heart.

That's... really sweet, Samus responded.

Yeah, but now it's my turn again, Jackie said. *How did you know you were trans? Was there a particular moment or did you always know?*

Oh my. Big question. Let me see.... Well, Metroid was one indication. At the end of the game, Samus takes off her helmet and you realize the anonymous bounty hunter you've been playing is really girl. I remember thinking that the reveal made so much sense, because I was a girl too, but no one saw.

You knew that young?

Yes and no. I really didn't have the language to express that sentiment, so I just forgot about it. When I was twenty-one or so I realized what the word trans meant. But it was still another year and a half before I accepted it.

Really?

Yeah. It's... weird, you know? We're not told we can change this aspect of ourselves. So I became really bitter about it. I remember staying online a lot—and I hate to admit this, but I was a troll. I was one of those people who would play games online and call people faggots and sissies and just be vile. And if Gamer Gate had happened back then, I know I would have been on the #notallmen side of the argument. Because I thought I wasn't like all men. I hated being seen as a man. And it took me getting into a really nasty argument with another female gamer to realize I hated her because I wanted to be her.

Jackie read the message two or three times. She didn't know what to say to any of it. It was so bizarre thinking of Samus as a bitter or mean person. She was so kind now. *She was worried about how cold my nose was.* How could Samus ever call anyone a faggot?

I'm sorry. Have I scared you off? Samus wrote a minute later.

No, no. Just letting it sink in. This is all so new to me.

It is for a lot of people. It's so hard to untangle our ideas of sex and gender from one another. Then it's even harder for some people to accept that your body is your own, and you can do with it what you want. Be it change your gender presentation or just get a lot of tattoos.

Jackie suddenly recalled the flash of ink on Samus's arm when they first met. *Do you have tattoos?*

Ah, you're not letting me ask questions! But yes, I do. That is all I will say.

Sorry, I'm skipping ahead. Ask me something.

Are you worried about being with me?

Jackie bit her lip. She wanted to throw her phone so she could avoid the answer. But with a sigh, she finally wrote. *Yes, I am. But not in the way you think.*

What way do you think I think? (Also: we're totally throwing our quid pro quo arrangement out the window, but that's cool.)

Jackie thought for a long time, even when she started typing, she wasn't sure if this was what she really wanted to say, or the only words that came to her about the issue. *I'm worried about being naked. I always am, usually, but this time it seems a bit weirder since our bodies are so different. At least, I think they are?*

After Jackie hit send, there was a long silence.

Jackie berated herself for being callous, then started to pace, her tea gone completely cold, before Samus replied.

All bodies are different, though. You know? Even when I thought I was gay, and I was with men, their bodies were all so different to me. Maybe that's a bad example, because well duh I'm trans, but get two cis people together and the same thing happens. All bodies are different. And really, we don't have to have sex. We can wait and wait and wait. I just... like you a lot. And I want to spend time with you. Doing whatever.

Jackie smiled. *Yeah, me too. About spending time with you. I have a lot of fun.*

Well, good. I'm glad we have that understanding. Hah. Now for some easier questions?

Definitely, Jackie wrote. *What's your favourite meal?*

Buffalo wings. And beer. Something like that—food you'd get at a bar on a late night. You?

Pizza. So late night food too.

Nice. Well, I have a couple more questions for you, like favourite colour and movie and everything in between, but I have to grade. You could tell me later, if you want.

Yeah, I understand. We have a date coming up. We could finish this conversation then.

We could do a lot of stuff then, Samus wrote. Jackie could see the other implications in the words, and for once, she wasn't afraid.

Yeah, definitely. Everything sounds good.

Then it's settled. Right now, though, I've got to

grade and focus on the future.

Yeah, Jackie replied. Her eyes flitted towards her bedroom door, where her half-finished projects still waited. *Me too. Goodnight.*

Goodnight.

Chapter Ten

"Fuck," Samus said.

"What's wrong?" Lindsey asked.

Samus tore her eyes away from her phone and the passive aggressive email. "I tried to book the theatre at the school for my fantasy class, but apparently the engineers need it more. So my reservation just got cancelled. Ugh."

"No way. That can't be right." Lindsey grabbed Samus's phone and read the email with wide eyes. "Good God. I can't believe they would literally kick you out a week before. And just because there is an engineering lunch? Why can't they move when you've been planning this for months?"

Samus balled her fists. This was not about her. She knew that for a fact. Whereas her normal response whenever she was rejected from a renter's application or a job interview outside academia was to chalk it up to the fact that she was trans and one of her references had slipped with pronouns, this wasn't the case with the sudden email cancellation. "Waterloo is a math and science school. They don't care about English as a discipline. They think we can do our presentations anywhere, so out we go."

"You can't, though. You were trying to organize this like an art gallery. For at least forty people, right?"

Samus nodded. Her study body capped at twenty-five, but there were several people who planned on bringing friends, partners, and parents to the final display. Samus's supervisor for her dissertation also wanted to see what she had been working on with her class, and he'd be bringing his wife. Then there was Jackie, who was supposed to be planning something to display as well. The guest list was growing and growing, and there was no way that the small classroom over the Environmental wing would hold everyone.

"We also need wall space and laptop space. One group made a film, some made games, and two girls I know for sure have a comic book they've framed some of the panels for," Samus added. "Fuck. I don't even know what to do."

"What time is it? The class date, I mean?"

"Next Wednesday at about three PM. It's the typical class time, but we were going to have the show last until at least seven, so a lot of people could wander through if they wanted. There's no exam for the class, so this is really the last time we all get to hang out before I disappear and grade for a month."

"Okay, that makes sense. Would it kill your students to move it to a Friday night?"

"I don't know. Why?" Samus furrowed her brow at Lindsey, who now had a devious smile on her face. "What are you planning?"

"Why not have it here?" Lindsey gestured around them at the Grad House. They were on the second floor, tucked away into one of the side rooms by the manager's office. Their fries were half-finished in front of them and they still shared a pitcher of Diet Coke. Beyond this small room, the Grad House actually had a spacious second floor with ambient lighting and comfy seats. If they moved some of the tables out of the way, and took down some of the kitschy art to replace it with student art, it could work. *Maybe.*

"You really think so?"

"Yeah, why not?" Lindsey said. "I mean, the Grad House hosts poetry nights and art shows. Why not an English class full of fantasy projects? So long as your students don't mind burritos and fries being sold at the same time?"

"We could have it on both floors?"

"Oh, yeah! Definitely."

Samus's heart stopped beating so erratically. She could see the first floor now, full of floral couches in the far room and a large bay window that let light inside to illuminate the art on the walls. They could put a projector in the main dining area, and keep the cafe section right by the window free for people to come in, sit and chat, and maybe eat a bit while viewing the short films. The upper floor could have the more personal exhibits, maybe even a game or two.

"That sounds perfect. You are such a lifesaver."

Lindsey waved away the compliment. She took a quick swallow of her pop before standing up. "Just let me ask Kelsey before we get too excited. I think he's next door doing the scheduling for the upcoming week, so we should have an answer fast."

"Will he go for it?"

"Probably. Having more people here means more revenue. I'll give him some details—actually, can you forward me that email? He hates the engineering side of the building just as much, and knowing the sob story will go really far."

"Uh. Sure." Samus forward the message to Lindsey then heard her phone buzz.

"Excellent. Thank you."

"Thank *you!*" Samus said. "Seriously, you're saving me so much time and trouble right now."

"Well, I may not be doing this entirely selflessly," Lindsey confessed.

"Oh?"

"Yeah. I may have a huge favour to ask when I get back. So keep thinking happy thoughts of me for now, yeah?"

Samus could only laugh. As Lindsey disappeared around the corner, she let out a deep breath. The final fantasy night would happen. It would be moved, but that would only give people some more time to practice and plan. Samus was halfway through typing an email to her students to give the updated information when Lindsey returned.

"And you're all set up. I have you booked at four until nine. Set up at three. So it's a little later than you may have wanted, but it's good to go."

"That's still perfect. Thank you." After adjusting some of the times, Samus hit send on her email, and leaned back into her chair. "Crisis averted, huh?"

"I *am* superwoman around here. But even I

need some help. So..." Lindsey picked up their pitcher of Diet Coke and topped up both their glasses in a professional, business-like tone. "Now for my favour: You remember my sister Nadia, right?"

Samus didn't really, but she nodded along. "Sure. What's the issue?"

"She's dragging me to her wedding dress fitting later on this week. We're gonna go to Niagara Falls after to check out the venue, too. I had no idea weddings needed so much work, but apparently they do. And she has a cat she can't get anyone to take care of, since her fiancé is going along with his bachelor friends the same weekend."

"So I'm looking after a cat? For a couple days? That seems really simple. Not to mention playing to my strengths." Samus grinned, already anticipating a giant ball of fur like the old tabby cat she had grown up with.

"Yeah, but this is a weird cat. So it may not be as straight forward." Lindsey pulled up her phone, swiping through a couple images until she found what she needed. She flashed Samus an image of a hairless sphinx cat with dark patches all over its body.

"This is Fluffy," Lindsey stated. "She looks like a chicken breast with arms and my sister thinks she's super clever for naming her Fluffy. But she needs to be bathed because she has no hair and apparently this breed loves the water. I don't really know. The thing looks like a giant rat to me, but apparently she was an expensive and spoiled rat, so she needs a lot of care and will whine a lot if she's not given it. I'm not really selling this well..."

"No!" Samus laughed a bit. "This is fine. Really. Kind of hilarious. But I think you're underestimating me. I can take care of cat. I mean, how bad could it be?"

"Famous last words. But thank you, seriously." Lindsey placed her phone down, so she could get up and hug Samus from the other side of the table. "You're a lifesaver. A superhero too."

"Naturally."

Lindsey shuffled back into the booth and wrote a quick text message to Nadia. "I think we'll see you on Friday morning. How does that sound?"

"Um." Samus thought of Jackie right away. "It's fine. Just let me make a new plan first."

"Good. I'll get us some more fries. On me."

Samus thanked Lindsey then pulled up a new message from Jackie. She grinned at their flirtations, full of heated suggestions and double entendres. *Now,* Samus wrote, *I'm not cancelling for Friday. Definitely not. Much too excited about seeing you again. But how do you feel about cats?*

~~*

As it turned out, Fluffy was a bit of a handful.

After she had been dropped off by Lindsey and Nadia, Fluffy spent most of her time hiding under Samus's bed. When Samus opened a can of Fancy Feast to lure her out, she was brave enough to be coaxed into the kitchen. She hissed at all the figurines that Samus had on her desk and in her entertainment unit before running back into the bedroom.

"Well, fine," Samus said. "You can stay there. See if I care."

Samus glanced at her microwave clock. *And all of this excitement before ten AM?* Jackie would be coming over at four so they could spend the evening together. She said she liked cats, so that wasn't going to be an issue. *But my exhaustion will be.* Since Fluffy was keeping Samus's room for herself, Samus grabbed a stack of reading for her dissertation and curled up on her living room couch. She was halfway through the first paragraph on the mechanics of video games before she passed out.

When she awoke, several hours later, it was to a sickly feeling of skin-to-skin on her arm.

"What the...?" Samus looked down to see Fluffy perfectly poised and content on her lap. "Oh, hello."

As Samus sat up on the couch, Fluffy made a few noises of disagreement. She jumped off the couch then doubled back to nestle next to Samus's legs. Samus reached down to pet Fluffy's head and neck, receiving a response of purrs. In spite of the weird feeling of Fluffy's skin, Samus had to admit she liked the cat. Now that she was adjusted, she seemed downright sweet.

"I'm actually gonna miss you in a few days, I think," Samus said.

Fluffy glanced up, purred a bit, then lay down and went right to sleep. Samus, not wanting to disturb her position, went back to reading—and then right to sleep again.

When her phone pinged at two in the afternoon, Samus realized she had completely lost track of her day. The message was from Lindsey, reminding Samus that the cat would need a bath the first night, especially after travelling to see her.

Her skin is oily, right? And apparently that gets worse when they're stressed, so, bath time! Thank you again. I will buy you video games when I return. Promise. Xoxox.

Samus sighed. Though Fluffy didn't look too bad, she knew that Lindsey was right. *And if I want to show you off to Jackie, then I have to bathe you right now.*

"Come on, girl," Samus said. She reached her arms down to pick up Fluffy. The cat was content to be carried all the way to the bedroom, but as soon as Samus stepped into the bathroom, Fluffy's claws came out. Then, as soon as Fluffy hit water, she mewled as if she was in pain.

"No water? I thought Lindsey said you loved it?"

Samus tried to lower Fluffy into the bath again, only to have the cat's paws create a giant splash in return. Once submerged, Fluffy walked around the bottom of the tub so fast that all the water spilled over the edge. Samus jumped back then grabbed some towels to soak up all of the mess. Fluffy ran around a few more times, dispelling the water, until it was significantly less full. Only then did Fluffy stop mewling and crying, and settle into her fate.

"Was that it?" Samus asked aloud. "Did you just want less water? Oh, man."

Samus mopped up more of the water. When she soaked up both of her towels, she left Fluffy alone as she went into the laundry room. Just as she grabbed another set of towels for her bathroom, there was a knock at the door. Samus braced herself for her downstairs neighbours complaining about a sudden dripping from her ceiling. Samus readied several apologies in her mind—only to forget all of them when Jackie was on the other side of the door.

"Oh. You! Hello."

"Hi. Sorry. Your neighbour let me in, so I came up when I found your name on the register downstairs. I'm a bit early, though, so I hope everything's okay."

"Yeah, of course. I'm just..." Samus glanced down at her top. Not only was it soaked through, but she was still wearing her laze-around-the-house clothing. No make-up (not that she really wore that much, anyway), and her hair wasn't done. "I'm just a bit thrown off today."

"The cat?" Jackie asked.

"The cat. Definitely. Everything's a bit wet right now." Samus bit her lip, realizing the subtle double entendre in her statement. *The pussy is completely wet. Oh, God. This is awful.* "But please, come in. The living room is fine."

Jackie slipped her shoes off at the front, along with her spring jacket. As she walked down the hall, her eyes darted around the small apartment, assessing the toys and models. She smiled when she spotted a few from *Firefly* and then a couple more from *Lord of the Rings.* Samus was so intent on watching Jackie, realizing just how much she missed her the past few weeks, she almost forgot that Fluffy was completely unsupervised.

"Oh, wow! Is this the limited edition set?" Jackie asked.

"Um. Actually—hold that thought. I think the cat may need me for a second."

"Oh, of course." Jackie stepped away from the Brandon Lee as *The Crow* figurine. "I can help with her, if you want?"

As if she could understand, Fluffy meowed from the bathroom. Jackie peered behind Samus's body then raised an eyebrow. "Wait. Is the cat in the bathroom?"

"Yeah. She's hairless, right? I thought I mentioned that."

"You did. I just thought all cats hated water?"

Samus laughed. "I can't believe I left this out of my messages. Today's been an experience in everything I thought I knew about cats. Apparently this breed likes water, though Fluffy likes to splash more than anything. She's probably destroying my towels or bathtub right now."

"Oh, my God. She's actually having a bath right now? I need to see this."

Samus extended her hand, leading Jackie down the hallway and into her bedroom with the en suite bathroom. Jackie's eyes didn't dart around as much as they did in the living area, which was a relief. Samus noted all her dirty clothing on the floor, including old pairs of underwear and her PJs.

With two people inside the bathroom, everything was super cramped. Fluffy stopped walking around and sat in the centre of the tub, staring at Jackie skeptically.

"Is she friendly?"

"Yes, but really, really fussy. She hissed at everything in my place for the first three hours she was here."

Jackie folded the toilet seat lid down so she could sit. She leaned her hands over the still-wet edge of the tub, extending a finger to Fluffy while whispering, "Hey, kitty, kitty..."

Fluff's skin was so wrinkly that Samus swore the cat furrowed her brow at Jackie. She leaned forward to sniff Jackie's fingers then licked one of them. The smile on Jackie's face was so wide, Samus couldn't look away.

"Oh, my *God*, this is so cute," Jackie exclaimed.

"I had no idea you loved cats. I would have sent you pictures."

"I don't, really. But Fluffy is a new thing. And I like new things."

"Oh?" Samus asked, a teasing tone in her voice. "I think I do too. As much as she's been a bit of a troublemaker, I like her."

"Good. I'm glad you were just busy earlier today."

"Were you texting me?" Samus tapped the front of her jeans to try and find her phone. Nothing. It was probably lost on the couch somewhere from when she had her nap. Several naps. Her cheeks reddened. "Sorry I didn't get back to you. Today's been..."

"Weird, I know. I'm just glad you didn't cancel. I brought the game, you know. But we don't have to play it. Especially since we're busy right now."

"Yeah, we are. But I wouldn't cancel. I've been waiting too long to see you." Samus knelt down on the tile floor, folding the towels underneath her so she didn't get her jeans wet. She extended a hand over Jackie's knee, her fingers tentative. When Jackie smiled, Samus knew everything was all right.

"I'm just sorry I lost track of time," Samus said. "And now I'm wearing crappy clothing and don't look good."

"Shh," Jackie said. "You're fine. Wonderful."

"Yeah?"

"Yeah."

When Jackie pressed their lips together, Samus moved into the action easily. She opened her mouth, allowing their tongues to touch. Samus inched closer, closing the distance between their bodies as her hands explored Jackie's skin. When Jackie's hand came to rest along Samus' jaw line, then to her hair, Samus grabbed Jackie's other hand and placed it over her chest.

Jackie made a sudden noise in her throat. She broke the kiss, leaning her head against Samus's. "Is this okay?" she asked, referring to her hand over Samus's chest. Samus's nipples grew hard.

"Yeah. I wouldn't have put it there if it wasn't. Are you okay?"

"Uh-huh."

When Fluffy meowed, they both giggled. Samus glanced over to the cat, splashing some water at her. "You be quiet. You got your turn."

Samus kissed Jackie again, their pace much faster and frantic. Jackie placed another hand over Samus's breasts, rubbing her thumbs along her nipples. Her shirt was thin, still damp from the water, and made Samus feel as if she were see-through. *I probably am see-through.* The thought that Jackie could almost see her naked didn't fill Samus with dread or worry, only pure excitement. But as they continued to make out, Flurry continued to meow. And then meow again.

Samus sighed. "I think I have to take her out of the bath and dry her off now unless I want her to run around my apartment like a fiend."

"Okay," Jackie said breathlessly. Her hands slid down from Samus's breasts to her waist. "We can keep doing this after though, right?"

"Definitely." Samus pecked Jackie one last time, before she scooped the cat out of the bathtub. Jackie held open a towel so they could catch and coddle Fluffy, and then let her loose in the apartment. Samus thought she saw Fluffy barrel down the hallway and start to sniff at Jackie's bag. She was worried for a moment then realized Fluffy's interest was most likely harmless.

"Seems like Fluffy also wants to play," Samus remarked.

"Uh-huh. I'll teach you how to play. But not now."

"Okay. What did you have in mind for now?"

The Big Reveal

Samus couldn't hold back her grin. They were in her bedroom, the light from the en suite illuminating a small pathway to the bed. Samus fought the urge to turn the light off, to surround themselves in darkness so the stripping part before sex would be easier. She knew that wasn't what Jackie wanted. It wasn't what Samus wanted, either. She knew that for sure now.

"Your shirt is wet," Jackie said pointing to a stain around Samus's belly.

Samus grabbed the edge of her shirt and pulled it off. Jackie's eyes moved from Samus's breasts to her tattoos along her arms. Reflexively, Samus displayed her inner arm so Jackie could see the outline of a lion underneath her armpit.

"You can touch it, if you want," Samus said after Jackie had been staring a while.

Jackie took a step closer before she traced her fingers over the finer edges of the line work. "What's it from? It looks familiar."

"It's technically my star sign, but I wanted to do something much cooler than just getting the astrological sign on my arm. So I had them model it after Aslan."

Jackie explored down the inked lion, right to Samus's elbow, before she touched Samus's bra line. Their eyes met before their lips did again. Samus moaned into Jackie's mouth, trying to encourage her to take off her clothing. Samus wanted to be seen, more than ever before, and she had a feeling that Jackie did as well.

When Samus felt the looseness of her bra being undone, she let out a small hiss.

"Is that okay?"

"Yes. God. More than okay," Samus insisted. She shucked off her bra, letting it drop to the ground. Before Jackie could step away and marvel at her chest, she tugged the edges of Jackie's T-shirt. "Can this come off?"

Jackie bit her lip. "Yeah, but... can I leave my bra on? Or can you not touch my breasts?"

"Sure," Samus said without question. "That's easy."

Jackie smiled. Samus helped to take off Jackie's T-shirt, but then stopped, allowing her to finish the rest. After a moment of thought, Jackie's sports bra came off too, revealing red-line imprints from the fabric against Jackie's tanned skin.

Jackie's breasts were small, her nipples already hard, but Samus didn't touch them. Instead, she linked her hands around the base of Jackie's back and held her close. Their lips pressed together again, Jackie's tongue more insistent than before. When she trailed kisses down Samus's neck, then over Samus's collarbone, Samus's cock twitch between her legs.

"Fuck," she gasped. Jackie's hands caressed her breasts, her tongue swirling around the nipple. "I need to sit. I need..."

Jackie backed away as Samus sat on the edge of the bed. Samus needed to untuck *so* badly. But she also didn't want to take her pants off and pressure Jackie to do the same.

"Are you okay?" Jackie asked, sitting next to Samus on the bed, her hand trailing over Samus's fingers.

"Yes, but... I need to take off my pants. I need to readjust myself."

Jackie nodded. As she kissed Samus, she also quieted whatever apprehension Samus had previously. After undoing her fly and inching down her jeans, Samus shifted. Her cock, painfully hard and wet, rubbed against the tight fabric of her boy-short underwear. Jackie's eyes flitted over the sudden bulge in Samus's underwear, but she didn't look scared or disgusted. She looked intrigued.

"Can I...?"

"Yes," Samus answered right away. She placed a hand on Jackie's chin, tilting their faces together as Jackie undid her own pants. Jackie broke the kiss to shimmy down to her jeans and the boxers she was wearing.

"I like your underwear," Samus laughed. "I think I used to have a pair like that."

"I like yours," Jackie said. "Because I think I used to have a pair like that too."

Samus laughed again then bit her lip. Jackie's palm pressed into Samus's thigh, and she spread her legs on command. Jackie, her face ashen and determined, positioned herself between Samus's pale thighs.

"Is this okay?" Jackie asked.

"It is for me. But what do only you want to do."

"I... don't know. I've never worked with a penis before." Jackie paused. "Can I call it that?"

"Yeah, but that's super technical. And really, I haven't worked with cocks much either. I have one, but... it's odd. I can do things with it, but I don't always like to."

"That's like me and my breasts, I think. Everyone always grabs them, and I'm kind of over it."

Samus smiled. She ran a hand over Jackie's face then leaned down to press their lips together. A chaste kiss soon became a heated make out session, and Samus's cock stained the front of her panties. Jackie seemed to notice right away, because her fingers brushed over the spot, then traced down to where Samus's balls were just behind the thin fabric.

"Fuck, you're so... wet."

"I am. It's a side effect of the hormones. I can have multiple orgasms now, too."

"Really? That must be great."

"Oh, it is." Samus licked her lips. Jackie stroked back towards Samus's shaft, then around the edge of the underwear. When she pressed inside it, her fingers against the skin, Samus let out a shudder.

"Do you want me to take this off?"

Samus nodded. Jackie made no attempt to take off her own boxers, and really, Samus was okay with that. So long as they were still together, still touching each other, she didn't care what else happened. Now naked, Samus sat back down on the bed, and Jackie remained between her legs. When she looked at Samus's cock too long, Samus pressed a kiss against her mouth.

"Don't do anything you're not comfortable with," Samus insisted.

"I want to try..." Jackie kissed down from

Samus's jaw to her breasts then hovered around her cock. Precome coated most of her dick, making it so she was super sensitive all around. Just Jackie's breathing was getting her completely overwhelmed, so when Jackie took her in her mouth, she nearly moaned and came right them.

"Fuck. *Fuck*." Samus pulled back and held onto Jackie's shoulders after a couple head bobs. She wanted to touch Jackie; to squeeze her breasts or something, but she held back. She ran her hand through Jackie's hair then whispered encouragements when she slowed.

"What do you like?' Samus asked as Jackie paused for a moment. "What do you want me to do?"

"Um..." Jackie reached down to her boxers, sliding them off her hips. Samus gazed at Jackie's round pubis and a triangle patch of dark hair which extended up towards her navel in a thin trail. Samus placed a finger over the hairline, following it down. Jackie's clit was already hard and pushing its way outside her lips. Samus used the flat of her thumb to coax it out more.

Jackie shuddered. "Your mouth."

"My mouth?" Samus asked. "I can do that. You'll have to come closer."

After another shudder, Jackie did just that. Now that they were both naked, everything was a lot less scary. Easy, even. Jackie lay down on the bed, her cheeks flushed red. Her small breasts moved up and down as she panted, her legs parted and wet. Samus settled between Jackie's legs, touching the clit with her thumb again before she reached out with a tongue to explore.

"Ohhh," Jackie moaned when Samus's tongue was more aggressive.

"Do you like things inside you?" Samus asked. "Should I use my fingers too?"

When Jackie shook her head, Samus withdrew. She repositioned herself, lifting Jackie's legs up a bit so she could lick her clit only. Her tongue swirled around the lips, pulling back some of the skin, before she swarmed over the clit again. Jackie moaned, her thighs squeezing Samus in closer. Samus fell into a rhythm that seemed to coax the most moans out of Jackie, licking with the flat of her tongue before pulling back. Jackie's hips bucked with each movement before she was shuddering.

"Oh, God," Jackie cried. "Fuck."

Samus pressed her face in closer, humming, before she felt a sudden shudder move through Jackie. Samus gasped around Jackie's clit, which seemed to trigger another sudden orgasm. Jackie moaned, almost crying out entirely, before she laughed.

Samus pulled her mouth away; she kissed Jackie's knees and inner thighs until she calmed down.

"Fuck," Jackie said. "That was... Oh, God."

"Good. I'm glad." Samus scaled up Jackie's body then kissed her on the mouth. Jackie's hands cupped Samus's tits, her fingers lingering on the nipples. Samus's cock touched Jackie's belly, and she reached out to grab her again.

"What do you like?"

"A lot of things really," Samus answered. "Do you want to put things inside me?"

Jackie grinned, biting her lip as she did. "What do you have?"

"Oh, lots of things." Samus's gaze fell on her drawer by her bed, filled with lube and toys and a lot of handbooks on good trans sex. Jackie followed her gaze, equally interested, and still flushed with arousal. Before she could move, Samus kissed her again, long and hard and deep.

The night had just started, and it was about to get *very* interesting indeed.

Chapter Eleven

Jackie couldn't stop thinking about it. As she stared at the ceiling in Samus's small apartment, she could still feel what it had been like to wear a strap on. It wasn't the first one she had worn one, far from it, but the way she felt with it on and with Samus was so, so different than all the other times.

But what was it? Maybe it was less the toy and more Samus, she finally decided. *Yeah, that was probably all it was.* Jackie turned over in the bed, wrapping an arm around Samus. She had a T-shirt and a pair of underwear on, but no bra on underneath. Jackie could feel the fullness of her breasts under her arm, and shuddered at how close they had just been. Jackie only wore her sports bra and boxers; her typical bedroom attitude.

Samus had her iPad propped on her legs, Netflix pulled up and streaming a TV show. Jackie wasn't even paying attention to the screen anymore, in favour of staring at the ceiling and trying to figure out her own thoughts. Now, with her head next to Samus, she liked the bright lights and theme song and allowed herself to be lost again.

"That's probably enough," Samus said when

the episode was over. "It's getting late. Are you going to stay?"

Jackie smiled. "I don't think any more buses are running, so definitely."

"Oh yeah? Just the buses keeping you here?" Samus asked playfully.

Before Jackie could answer, Fluffy jumped back up on the bed and walked between the two of them. Jackie reached out and petted the cat's head.

"Yeah, just the buses and the cat. That's it."

Samus laughed. When Fluffy padded down to the bottom of the bed, where the spare blanket had been tossed, Jackie moved in closer to Samus to whisper in her ear. "No, not just those reasons. I'm... having a really good time."

"Oh yeah? Good. Because we haven't really had much of a chance to catch up. You know what I was doing today, but what were you up to?"

Jackie sighed. "Working on the dress my mom wanted. But then I gave up."

"Why?

"It's just not me. Doesn't fit. So I was working on something for your fantasy night sequence."

"Were you?" Even in the low light, Jackie could see how happy Samus was. "I'm so glad. I told you about the new plans for it, right?"

"Definitely. Is it okay if I bring Alicia along to the show?"

"Totally. Bring whoever—we have the space now." Samus grinned again then bit her lip. "I know I shouldn't put too much pressure on my students, but I really hope they come away from this course with something good."

"Something better than an A?"

"Yeah. I want them to actually learn and then apply this in their lives. So many people—like the engineers that kicked us out of our space—think English is pointless or too simple. But it's not, and I want this art show to prove it. I'm still convinced fantasy can change someone's life."

"How so?" Jackie asked. "I think you explained it to me before, but can I hear it again?"

"Oh, you're so good to humour me." Samus laughed. "But okay. I called the course Imagining the Future and Negotiating the Past, right? Because we have to negotiate our past in order to write something about it. But writing is also about imagining the future. In a way, most writing, even if it's set in contemporary times, is still about imagining what is possible. And until you imagine it, it can't be real. So a fantasy is something that is necessary in order to go on with living, almost." Samus paused. "Am I making sense? It's kind of late and I'm still in sex-mode, so of course the only fantasy I can think of is sexual—but hey. Those are important too."

Jackie laughed. "No, that totally works. Even sex fantasies can change someone's life, right? I mean, I didn't even know I could like women until I saw it on TV, then I realized just how much I wanted to do it too."

"*Exactly*. We don't know what our options are sometimes until we see them. Even if dragons or elves or whatever aren't real, we have at least been given a glimpse into something that could be real. In another possible life, in another world, another time. Just because it isn't happening right here doesn't mean it couldn't."

"Yeah," Jackie said. "I like that explanation. I think I've been working on something similar."

"Oh yeah? For the show?"

"And for me, in general. *Hack the Planet* doesn't have any male hackers. But I always wanted to be one when I cosplayed, so I'm creating a new one. Maybe if I pitch it to the company, they'll add him to the deck. And if not, then I still have something cool I've made."

Samus's beamed. "That's great. It totally fits with what we're doing."

"Yeah? So you'd pass my proposal?"

"Totally. I'd return it with no corrections and give you the green light. For real. I'm sure it'll look great in the fantasy showcase."

"Well, cool. Thank you. I'm still not done. Still not even really sure where it's going yet."

"It doesn't have to have a proper ending," Samus added, "if that's what you're worried about. Not even some of my students will have it all figured out yet."

"I know. But... it's important. For me, at least, to have an ending. I feel like I've been working on it a long time now."

Samus nodded and squeezed Jackie's arm. Tender, encouraging. "Well, be sure to tell me when you find out."

"I will." Jackie leaned over to kiss Samus. The embrace lingered until exhaustion overwhelmed Jackie and she pulled back. "Tomorrow, I promise,

I'll teach you how to play."

"Definitely. But tomorrow. So goodnight, Jackie."

"Goodnight."

Jackie kissed Samus once more before the bedside light shut off and plunged them into darkness. Samus fell asleep within a matter of minutes, her snores rhythmic beside Jackie. Jackie stared at the ceiling. Her thoughts about her past and her future continued to race for about an hour before she finally fell asleep.

~~*

In the morning, Samus was good to her word. Over coffee, the two of them finally learned how to play *Hack the Planet*.

"Only three months in the making," Jackie said as she dealt out the cards.

"Has it really been that long?"

Jackie nodded. She remembered the first day of the semester, walking into the wrong classroom, and then the brutal snow storm. Three months ago—and only a few more weeks until graduation.

"Man, time has flown by," Samus said. "But a happy three months, right? Can I say that?"

"Yeah." Jackie smiled. "And same to you."

After a short intro round, Jackie brought out the bigger threats and upped the amount of cards they could hold per turn. After another hour, the first game was over.

"This was really simple," Samus stated. "And a

lot of fun. Thank you."

Jackie beamed. She picked up the cards on the coffee table and shuffled them again. "Time for another round?"

"Definitely," Samus said. "And this time, I'll win."

Chapter Twelve

"Do you have everything?"

Samus turned to face Lindsey. She was dressed in her typical tight black jeans and a collared shirt, but Samus noted the button on the lapel for *Dragon Age*. Lindsey, who was typically a modernist scholar, was trying to fit in with the fantasy crowd at the Grad House in the only way she could.

"You look good," Samus said. "I like the Dorian and Cullen tribute."

"Please, it's nothing special. I only play games as a way to check out when I study for comp exams. But you didn't answer my question: Do you have everything? Or do you need me to be errand boy for you?"

"I think I'm fine..." Samus glanced around at the Grad House. Several of her students had already shown up and were standing next to their paintings or game, talking to the other students who had wandered in. Kelsey, the main manager, brought out a large pile of nachos on the house and a few other waiters who were working that night brought out drinks. Music swelled from the upstairs viewing area, followed by uproarious laughter as students were already diving into their games.

Though it was barely seven, Samus had to say that the night was a success. She knew that every student but one had handed in their final assignment (and that one student was notorious for not handing anything in on time but showing up anyway). Early in the afternoon, students arrived to set up their final assignments and Samus only had to call for Kelsey's help once—and that was only to get a ladder so they could hang a particularly long painting on the wall. Now that Lindsey was there, and each student had their own plus one guest, there was only partying left to do. *Grading too, but I'll get to that eventually.* There were three weeks before those grades needed to be official, anyway.

"Yeah, I'm great. Thanks so much for helping me put this together."

"Nah-uh. That was all you. I just made sure Kelsey gave you free nachos." Lindsey ushered them both to the free food, scooping a large dollop of sour cream onto her chip. "So what student work do you want to show off first?"

"Um. Truthfully, Jackie's."

"Oh. Is she coming? And more importantly, is she being graded?"

"No, no grading. Though that could be a fun fantasy," Samus said, grinning. "But she's supposed to come. I thought I saw her earlier, but nothing yet."

"Not even for set up?"

"No..." Samus glanced at her watch, then at her phone. There was one message from Jackie, which seemed stiff and awkward. *Everything starts at four or five, right? Sorry I wasn't at set-up. Work stuff. I promise I'll give you something before the end big night. What I wanted to do... kind of spiraled out of control. But I promise. I'll bring something for you.*

I hope you'll hang around, too. Remember all work and no play makes Jack a dull boy.

"Nothing yet?" Lindsey asked when Samus had replied.

"No, nothing yet. But she's coming. Just working extra hard, I guess."

"Maybe you should give her extra credit. You know." Lindsey tried to wink, but utterly failed. The two of them chuckled for a moment then ordered drinks. When Samus glanced down at her phone again, she noticed that Jackie had seen the message, but didn't respond. *Odd*. Samus didn't have much time to over-think the response before Lindsey tugged on her arm again.

"Did I tell you about that girl?"

"What girl?"

"The one I met!"

Samus eyed Lindsey carefully. "I thought you weren't into women?"

"Well, no, but... this one is so cool. I think I definitely have a girl-crush. She's also into Virginia Woolf, in grad school, and writes poetry! She's been published. And not like, student-published or one of those publishing sweepstakes scams. Like, legit published."

"Whoa, really? Anything I would have heard?"

"It's not speculative poetry, so no, probably not. But it's super-cool, right?"

"Definitely cool. How did you two meet?"

"At my sister's bridal shower! I forget how she knows Nadia, but we both felt super awkward so we talked about the modernists all night. Total nerds, but I love it."

"Great. I'm so happy for you." Part of Samus panged with jealousy that Lindsey was showing so much interest in another woman (and, in spite of what Lindsey said about this being platonic, Samus knew that gleam in her eye too well), but Samus shook it off. *You have Jackie now. At least, I think I have Jackie...* Samus scanned the Grad House once again, still not spotting Jackie in the crowd. Lindsey followed her gaze.

"Hey. Are you worried?"

"Maybe a little."

"Is there any reason to be? Did you two have a fight?"

Samus shook her head. "No, things have been going ridiculously well."

"Then don't read too much into her being late. There are so many reasons why she could be. It's the end of term, right? And you said she was graduating, so she's probably just super busy. You both are, right?"

"Right, I know." Samus nodded. That was true. They hadn't really seen much of one another, aside from quick coffee dates on campus, since the blissful weekend they spent with Fluffy. It was almost a relief to have that cat, since she was so ridiculous she allowed them to bond over something that wasn't about school or their typical nerdy topics. "I'm just really sick of school fucking up relationships."

"Oh, sweetie. It's not that bad. You'll finish this semester and then the summer will start. And you're not teaching then. Things *always* get easier in the summer." Lindsey reached a hand for Samus's shoulder, regarding her sympathetically.

"You have a point. What about you? Is your summer looking suitably idyllic in a John Hughes type of way?"

"Oh, please. I have to teach another semester with Bethany Wright again!" Lindsey took a sip of her drink. "And there's Nadia's wedding."

"But you'll have your girl, then, I'm supposing."

Lindsey smiled. "Maybe... but she's not my girl."

"Not yet. Her name?"

Lindsey sighed, but her smile was still present on her lips. "Alison."

"Nice. I'll remember it."

When Lindsey changed the topic to work again, Samus nodded along, only half-listening. She supposed Lindsey did have a point about the summer always being so much easier. And there was no use being upset about school keeping Jackie and them apart, especially when she couldn't control it. This fantasy night was for Samus as much as it was her students, and she needed to start getting into the spirit. After Lindsey was done complaining about her exam committee, Samus swung her arm around her and geared them both towards the staircase.

"Enough chit-chat. How about a game?"

"Oh no!" Lindsey squealed playfully. "I'm here

for art and support. That's it."

"Come on, don't be a spoilsport. Wait until you see this game they invented." Samus turned into the room at the top of the stairs that was already buzzing with activity. "It's like D&D on steroids. You'll love it. Hey, Steve. Do you need another player?"

~~*

Almost an hour passed before Samus heard her name being called. When she did, it was Sally, one of her students in second year. She stood with her hands folded primly, her long dark hair pulled tight on the top of her head in a ponytail. Her voice was soft, and she seemed utterly distraught for even bothering Samus while she was playing a new card game someone in her class had created using all the characters from Sir Gawain and the Green Knight.

"Can you look over what I've done? I know you're super busy, but I want to be sure it was part of the assignment."

"I'm sure it's fine. I accepted your proposal, remember? I had you guys all do a proposal to make sure everyone was on the same page," Samus said. She handed her cards to Lindsey, who took over her place in the game eagerly. "But lead the way."

"I know. You're probably right. I wanted to do Urban Fantasy, but I'm worried it didn't work. I don't know. Can you still look?"

"Of course. That's what I'm here for." Samus

assured Sally again, but she knew it would do no good until she actually saw the project. Most of the art was on the top floor, along with many of the games and some short films. Samus expected that Sally—who was always meeting in her office hours—was nervous because her stuff probably wasn't as interactive as the other students, and she worried she had done the assignment wrong.

"Which project is yours again?"

Sally gestured to the corner piece. Already, Samus could see the wild amounts of colour used. A rainbow stretched across the top of one small canvas, followed by ten chalices. A family with two black parents and a child were at the centre. Samus noted there was an inch or two at the bottom framed away with the number ten in Roman numeral written there.

"This is nice," Samus said. "But how about you explain to me what you've done first?"

Sally shifted from side to side, worried her hands together. "I wanted to do urban fantasy, right? But I had a hard time imagining what I wanted to do without borrowing everything. I know you said we could borrow, but we had to tweak it substantially. So I did this tarot card—ten for prosperity in cups—because that was the first one I pulled out of the deck, and I worked on adapting it for an urban fantasy setting."

Sally gestured towards another framed image. This one had three men in business suits posed in the same way the family was with the cups. Only in this image, the ten chalices were now discs, and the men were clearly in a business meeting of some kind.

"This is the ten of pentacles," Sally explained. "But in a more urban or modern setting. I ended up doing all four of the tens in the tarot deck. Some paintings have a more antiquated swords and sorcery feel to the fantasy, while others are more urban fantasy. Is that... okay? I know someone else re-imagined an entire deck, but since my pieces were bigger, I didn't want to have to do all of them. Does it make sense?"

Samus's eyes scanned the other two works. The ten of swords depicted someone flat on their back on a massage table. The swords were transformed into acupuncture needles that lined up the man's spine; the background was filled with lotus flowers. The ten of wands depicted a sage-like crone who held an arm full of magical wands. She gave each one out to children as they passed by her small cottage in the middle of what looked to be an enchanted forest.

"Can I ask one question, Sally?"

Sally's eyes were wide, but she nodded.

"I get why you picked the first ten, but why keep the theme?"

"Because when I researched the cards more, I realized most of the tens meant completion in some way and this was the end of our course. I wanted to get all the suits in the deck as well, which correspond to all the elements. Is that okay?"

"Yes," Samus said, smiling. "This is fine."

"Really?"

"Yeah. Of course. I just wanted to be sure

there was a reason behind the tens, and you weren't just randomly picking."

Sally smiled, clearly relieved. Samus noted a small crowd of her students gathered around herself and Sally. Though Samus wasn't anticipating turning this exhibition into a lecture, she could see everyone wanted some kind of statement about the night and what they had done. Samus scanned the room and spotted Lindsey in the corner with another drink in her hand. Then Samus spotted another bob of black hair on the stairs. *Jackie? Did she finally make it?* Samus grinned.

"So, now that everyone is gathered here, I want to say thank you," Samus began. "Everything that I've seen tonight is fantasy in some way or another. Whether it's a game, a video, or a painting. Even if some of these projects build on existing worlds, like the tarot cards or D&D, each one of you has taken that world and expanded it for yourselves. You've made your own fantasy within it, and therefore, you've made something new.

"I was talking to someone recently about how nothing is possible unless we imagine it first. That goes right down to the very practical things like vaccines and bridges and cell phones, then to the impractical things like a unicorn. At one time, all dreams were seen as impossible. But with a bit of thought, time, and imagination, good things can happen."

"But what about the unicorn?" someone asked, laughing. Samus could tell right away it was

Chris, the guy who never handed anything in.

"Well, the unicorn is still important. Because it's the emotion behind that fantasy that becomes real. We all know *The Last Unicorn*, right?"

A few students gasped, while others murmured and nodded.

"Exactly," Samus said. "That emotion is real. So while the horse with a horn on its head doesn't exist, the emotion it evokes creates something in it. Wonder or whatever; it doesn't matter, as long as it brings people together. And Sally, your pieces more than anything, are pieces about mood. The business men in suits can be magical and mysterious, because they're thinking of their fortune in the same way Bilbo does. Of course they are. So they count."

Sally beamed under the direct praise. Samus could see another question behind her eyes (*does this mean I got an A?*), but she didn't want to answer it now. She didn't want to lecture anymore, either, so she tried to turn it over to everyone else.

"Now, speaking of emotions, you all should go around and congratulate your peers. You need to tell people when they've affected you in some way, or else how are they going to know? So mingle among groups you haven't talk to before. Leave nice comments on pieces of paper if you can't find the creator, and basically, enjoy yourselves tonight. You all deserve it. Have a good night, guys."

There was some chatter and a few scattered claps. No one got on the table and saluted Samus like *Dead Poets Society*, but she never wanted that anyway. As she wandered back over to Lindsey, she watched how students turned to one another and started to talk. Even Sally, normally super shy, eventually linked hands with Steven and played a game.

"How are you doing, Linds?" Samus asked. When Lindsey worried her lip, Samus faltered. "Was I too overdramatic back there? You can tell me—I won't be offended."

"Oh, no. That was sweet, actually. But Jackie just left."

"What? She didn't even say hello?" Samus's heart panged. Lindsey extended a file folder she had in her hand with *J. Vasquez* written across it. "Wait. What's that?"

"From Jackie. Which is the odd thing. She came up to me and gave me this, listened to you talk for about two minutes, but then ran the other way."

"That *is* odd. Maybe she's just tired..." Samus got out her phone and sent Jackie a text. *Everything okay? I wish you had stayed. I wanted to hear more about your piece.*

"So what is this?" Lindsey asked. "Can I look?"

"Um. Probably her project." Samus retrieved the file folder from Lindsey and opened it up so they both could view the sketches. There were several detailed plans for a suit in several different colours and a skin-tight body suit that resembled what some of the hackers in *Hack the Planet* wore. "Definitely her project. She did some stuff for a game we both like."

Lindsey nodded, completely absorbed in the

pieces. As Samus continued to flip through the sketches, she realizes these weren't just sewing patterns but complete character design. The last image was of someone called Jack Vice, a new hacker. His dark hair was coifed into a mohawk, and he wore a tight blue T-shirt with dark pants with lightning bolts by the ankle. His skin was tanned and he wore a nice pair of sunglasses over his small nose. *He's kinda cute,* Samus thought. *Just like...*

"That looks like Jackie," Lindsey stated. "Did she draw herself into the world?"

"I don't think so. Or... *Oh.*" Samus sighed. She flipped back to the beginning of the images and went through it from the start. And she understood. All the conversations she and Jackie had been having online came back in a wave. *Of course. It all makes perfect sense now.* Jackie hadn't been asking a million questions about transgender identity because she was worried about Samus. She was asking a million questions because she was worried about herself. If she even was a she anymore. *Oh, of course.*

Samus didn't know how she had been so blind. All the signs were there, if she wanted to see them. *No wonder she's not here tonight.*

"Uh-oh," Lindsey said. "What's going on? You just turned white."

"Nothing. I just... I think I have to go. Is that okay?"

Lindsey shrugged, holding her drink. "Depends. Can I take over as the leading lady of the night?"

"Sure. Just don't terrorize my students, okay?

There's only another hour of this, anyway."

"And then clean up," Lindsey pointed out.

"Right. Well, if you could do that..."

"Of course. Go rescue your girl."

Samus paused, but didn't bother correcting Lindsey. Instead, she gave her a hug. "Thank you for cleaning up. You're great."

"Obviously." Lindsey nudged Samus towards the door. "Good luck!"

"Thank you," Samus said. "I may need it."

Samus turned toward the exit and headed into the night.

Chapter Thirteen

Jack stared at the text message he had sent three hours ago. Really, three hours and four minutes ago. He glanced around the lobby of the theatre as one of the movies finished. A sea of people crossed in front of his bench just outside the Purple Fruit Cafe, which shared space with the Zebra Independent Theatre House. Jackie hadn't been here in such a long time; not since his mother had tried to make him wear a dress when attending his brother's wedding two years ago. He laughed at the memory now.

How did I not see this ages ago? he wondered. When he reread the email he had sent Alicia explaining everything, he felt another wave of relief wash over him. Alicia knew—or would know—as soon as she decided to finally pick up her phone.

> *Hi Leesha,*
>
> *Okay. This sounds like a serious email. It is. But don't worry, nothing is bad and I'm fine and I want to still have our business and make cool stuff together. But I'm going to need to change a few things first. One is*

that I can't be a "business woman"; as soon as we started to plan for this, I realized that was how people would see me. And maybe this is just Samus influencing me, maybe this is a phase, and maybe I'll feel better after saying all this and things can go back to normal, but I don't think so.

The fact is, I think I'm trans. So I think I really should be a boy. The more I think about myself as a he/him in my mind, the better I feel. The more I start to imagine myself as a guy in the future, it doesn't become scary. Well, it does, because if this trans feeling is real then it means a lot of doctors and possibly bigotry, so that's less cool. But I would rather face that than have to deal with being a business woman. Or a woman at all.

So yeah. You're technically the first person I'm telling because I'm still testing this out. But I'm a guy. I'm going to start to go by Jack instead of Jackie (but I still like that name way, way better than Jacqueline), and it would be awesome if you started to use male pronouns. Anything else, we can talk about! For sure! I may not be home until late tonight, but email me

when you get this. Or call. Or whatever.
   Take care, Jack.

Jack signed. He still did like the name Jackie—it seemed more neutral than anything—but he was also enchanted with the name Jack. He wasn't sure if it would be for Jackson or Jonathan, but again, he knew he'd figure it out. The hard part was telling the first person, and now that Alicia was out of the way, he had a few more important people to go.

When he glanced up again, the people coming out of the theatre passed by and a familiar face greeted him on the other side.

"Hi," Samus said. "I had a feeling I'd find you here."

"Hey." Jack shifted on the bench, moving his backpack between his legs to create more room for Samus. Samus sat down gingerly, but kept several inches between their bodies. "Hey, so...I'm sorry I didn't stay at your fantasy thing. How was it?"

"Fine, really. I missed you, but Lindsey showed me your art."

"I figured she would. Did you... did you like it?" Jack waited, biting his lip. He desperately wanted everything to be super-clear as soon as he gave Samus the drawings. Really, he wished Samus had sat him down and told him he was trans. He thought he exhibited all the symptoms and signs. But just because she was trans didn't mean she understood him and what was going on in his mind. Even if he thought he was being super clear about it all.

When Samus was quiet for a while, Jack asked, "Should I just tell you?"

"Yes. I think you should. Guesswork gets people hurt."

Jack nodded. "Well, I realized while doing the work for your course that I've been an idiot."

"You're not an idiot."

"I've only ever had male avatars. I've played men in books or video games or movies my whole life. I freaked out trying on a dress. I don't let you touch my breasts when we have sex. Isn't that... so obvious?"

"No. Because those things don't make someone trans."

"What does then?"

"I really don't know. I want to say dysphoria, but that's the medical diagnosis. I don't like thinking that it's only pain that makes me who I am."

"But there is something there," Jack stated. "There's something to that diagnosis. It's definitely not the be-all and end-all of being trans. But I did kind of feel shitty before and didn't understand why."

"Yeah, but that's the past. It's really the future that makes me who I am. At least, that's what I think. And I've told you my theories on that enough."

"Yeah, but I like your theories. And that's what helped me the most. Your class made me realize that I needed to imagine it before it could happen. And now I think I want it to happen. I think... I want to be a guy. I am a guy. As soon as I thought it, it was true, more or less."

"Yeah, I know that feeling." Samus laughed a bit. After a moment of silence, she reached over to hold Jack's hand in hers. "So why did you run away?"

Jack sighed again. He felt so maudlin, but he could be right now, right? He deserved it, especially when it felt as if he was starting everything from scratch. "I think I was worried."

"About what?"

"I don't know. That you'd run away first. You wouldn't like me anymore. Think I was copying or something."

"I like you because you're you. And I can like you as a guy. I'm bisexual, remember? I know I joke around that I'm gay all the time, but that's really because I usually prefer women. But I do like guys, too. I like you, of course, and you're a guy."

"Oh. Right. Well, that's good. I still like you. A lot, actually."

"Do you now?" Samus smiled. She inched closer, and Jack held her hand even tighter. When he nuzzled her shoulder, she tapped his chin so their mouths met. The kiss was chaste, more out of comfort than anything else.

"I like you a lot, probably too much so soon." Samus chuckled. "I'm going to need to know what to call you. My boyfriend?"

"Definitely," Jack said, liking the sound of it so much more than girlfriend.

"And I should use he/him pronouns?"

"Yeah."

"Okay. Easy. But your name? What do I call you now?"

"Jack." He nodded. *Yeah, it sounded so much better.* "Jackie is okay, too, but I think I prefer Jack. I'm not sure if I want Jackson or Jonathon yet, but I have time, I figure."

"You do. And you can change your mind."

"I can?"

"Oh yeah. The myth of sudden transformation is such bullshit. I stayed in a strange in-between area trying to decide whether or not I wanted to go the nerdy route and be Samus or Samantha or even something like Caroline. I considered that for a long, long time before I ever did anything legally."

"Huh. I can't imagine you as a Caroline."

"Neither could I. But sometimes it really does take a while to find the right balance. As much as doctors insist, not everyone realizes when they're three years old, either."

"Hah," Jack said. The laughter hurt his chest. "I'm fucking twenty-five, and I just realized."

"That's still super-young. *Super*-young. I've met women in their forties and fifties who cried when they realized there was a word for what they were."

"Wow," Jack said. It was all he could say for quite some time. Samus remained by his side, watching as another movie was let out. Her thumb rubbed against his own, and when Jack's phone went off, he didn't want to let her go.

"Is that yours or mine?" Samus whispered a moment later when it buzzed again. "I think it's yours."

"It is. Probably Alicia. I told her in an email."

"Oh. Do you want me to read it first? Or together?"

"Together."

Jack reached into his pocket and pulled out the phone, touching the email screen before he could double-back. When the first words were "*OH MY GOD I LOVE YOU SO MUCH,*" he knew he'd be fine. Jack stopped reading, choosing to rest his head on Samus's shoulders instead.

"She's fine," Samus declared when she had reached the end. "You have nothing to worry about, except maybe a long conversation with her later to explain some more stuff. Juts terminology and things, so if she ever gets a million questions from other people—and she will—then she'll be prepared."

"Right, okay. But later," Jack emphasised. "I don't even want to think about telling anyone else. Like my mom, or..."

"Shhh." Samus placed her fingers close to Jack's mouth. She kissed him again, lingering in the embrace for quite some time, before she pulled away to whisper in his ear. "How about we go to my place? I think I may have a surprise for you."

Chapter Fourteen

When Jack got to Samus's apartment, he was still surprised there wasn't a cat anymore. "I miss Fluffy," he stated as he stepped inside.

Samus laughed. "I know, right? I'm thinking of getting a cat now because I miss her. Not a hairless one, though. Too far out of my budget, but maybe a nice shelter cat."

Samus walked into her kitchen, flicking on the lights as she did. Jack noted the dishes in the sink, the laptop computer still plugged in at the table, and notes stacked all around. Samus seemed to follow Jack's gaze. She shrugged.

"What can I say—the end of term is fun for everyone. But at least I don't have to teach in the summer. I'm still dissertation writing, but it'll be better because I can work in my PJs if I want. Want some tea? I think we need some tea."

Jack nodded. Samus got out Lemon-Honey herbal tea and two large mugs.

"I was looking forward to summer," Jack said, "but now I don't know because of this whole thing."

"Hey. Don't get ahead of yourself. I know it seems really, really overwhelming... but one step at a time, okay? You're already doing well."

"Sure, whatever you say."

"Now, now. Don't get too cynical so soon on me." Samus set up the kettle then leaned on the counter. "And don't let the transition become your life. It's the newbie mistake everyone makes.

"I'll keep that in mind." When the water boiled and the tea was steeping, Jack asked, "Have I told you about the business that Alicia and I are going to open?"

"A little bit, but tell me more. And come, let's have our tea in the bedroom. Just to talk, I promise."

Jack grinned. He liked the fact that Samus, when not burdened with grading or other class obligations, would spend all day in bed. It was her safe place, her sanctuary, and he liked that he was invited back there. He imagined she'd probably even write her dissertation in bed, if she could only find a way to properly balance her laptop and all the books she'd need.

As Jack followed Samus into her room, then under the covers, he continued to relay some details about the business he and Alicia planned on opening.

"She has a cosmetology degree, and a full-time position in a salon, and she's going to keep doing that. But we're going to start a cosplay commissions business where she can be hired out at cons for make-up, and I can do the designing. It's still a really small venture right now, and you know, I'll probably have to get a real job, anyway. I did get a call back for the fabric store, so maybe that will end up working out. But I like the idea of being excited about something beyond the nine-to-five doldrums."

"I hear that," Samus said. "What are you going to call your business?"

"Just Your Size. We're still working on business card designs. I was thinking that the next time I see my mom, I tell her about the business first, then that I'm trans, so she can only pick one thing to be mad at. Right?"

Samus rolled her eyes a little. "No one's going to be mad. No one should be mad."

"In an ideal world, yeah..."

"I know. It's really hard to not expect the worse. But trust me on this. Don't act like it's a big deal, and maybe your mom will surprise you."

"And if she doesn't?"

"Then you have me." Samus curled her hand around Jack's free one. She squeezed it, encouraging him. He complained a bit more, spilling out his worst fears and having Samus combat them each time. It wasn't long before he realized his tea was warm.

"I'm sorry. I should really stop talking."

"No. I'd rather hear about all of this. But can I show you something that I think may help?"

"Yeah, sure! Is this your surprise? Please show me." Jack took a couple swallows of tea then set the mug down on Samus's bedside table as she got up. Samus walked into her closet, talking as she searched around the back.

"So I got my MA when I was still completely unaware that I was a woman. I had to go to parties, convocation, and get my pictures taken for the department website. My parents got me this suit for all these events so I appeared professional. But it was while I was doing all of this events that I realized I couldn't do it anymore. That the suit I was wearing would be my last one. And here it is."

Samus stepped out of the closet. She held a charcoal grey suit in her hands; slim or narrow fit, with a teal tie and matching silk pocket square. From what Jack could recall of his late night trolling on suit websites, this design was Ralph Lauren. He let out a low breath.

"That's... beautiful."

"I know, right? The fabric is impeccable. And I like this suit. I really think it's pretty, but on me? No. Absolutely not. When I was getting rid of my clothing during the transition, I kept this one. I used to think it was because the suit had become symbolic, but now I know it's just because I thought it was gorgeous. Just not for me. So really, I'm pretty sure I kept this so I could find someone that this suit would look gorgeous in. And then give it to them."

"Wait. You're giving this to me?"

"Yes. You'll probably have to take some of it in, since you're way skinnier than me, but you can adjust it all you want. I don't want the suit anymore, and it would look fantastic on you."

Jack opened his mouth, completely flabbergasted. He tried to say thanks, but started to cry instead. He placed a hand over his mouth then started to shudder as tears welled up and spilled over onto his cheeks. Samus placed the suit on the back of a chair before she wrapped her arms around Jack on the bed.

"I'm sorry," Jack said. "I'm being ridiculous again."

"No. It's fine! I cried when Lindsey bought me something with my name on it once. It was so pink and girly and no one had ever done that for me before. It can be emotional. It's ... really hard. It's kinda like crying at the end of a really good film or book, because you realize that it happened and it's great but now you have to move on with your life."

"Yeah." Jack nodded, his lip still trembling. The feeling of moving on was horrible, like a lump in his throat. In some moments, when he realized he was trans, he wanted to push it away because it meant he had to change the way he was currently living his life. Other nights, when he realized he was trans, he felt awful because it meant that his life as a girl had been a waste. But the life he had before *wasn't* a waste. His former life was a part of a weird journey, and like anything in fantasy, the quest needed to occur before he could go home again.

"Thank you," Jack said. "I really, really like it."

"You sure? My style doesn't always mesh well."

"Hey. I don't even know what my guy style is yet. So this can be the first step towards me figuring it out."

"Definitely. So go on," Samus said, gesturing towards the suit. "Try it on."

Chapter Fifteen

Jack was like a kid playing dress-up in his father's old clothing. The suit's shoulders were too big and the pants were too wide around the waist. *But I can fix all this*, Jack thought. *I can definitely fix all this.*

"Don't leave me in too much suspense," Samus pleaded on the other of her bathroom door side. "Let me see. When you're ready. Hopefully tonight at some point. It's already pretty late..."

Jack laughed. An honest, genuine laugh. He had never felt so good in any set of clothing—except for maybe the Julian Howard cosplay. *This time it's not a cosplay. This time, it's real.*

"I'm ready," Jack said.

Jack's hand fumbled on the doorknob once before stepping out. Samus's gaze flitted over the entire ensemble at least twice without revealing any emotion. Then she smiled. Wide and big.

"Well, that wasn't quite as dramatic as most big reveals. But I think it looks good. It suits you, that's for sure."

When Samus realized the pun she just made, she burst out laughing. Jack soon followed. He closed the distance between their bodies, placing his hands on her waist.

"Do I look like a little kid playing dress up?"

"Nah. You look really happy. That's what matters. Until, you know, the stores open and we can go shopping again."

Jack nodded, not saying much else.

"We don't have to go shopping tomorrow," Samus added quickly. "We can stay here. All day. In bed. In fact, let's do that. Because I think I really need to get reacquainted with you."

"Oh yeah? Is that so?"

"Yeah." Samus grinned as she placed her hands over Jack's on her waist. She gave a quick tug, and pulled them both onto her unmade bed. As Jack fell on top of her, their mouths crashed together. The kiss was rushed and hurried, teeth catching on lips, before Samus placed her hands on Jack's face and steadied both of them. Jack slid his tongue next to Samus and she did the same. As they made out, Jack trailed his hands over Samus's neck and breasts, rocking into her. Samus moaned at the friction. Jack felt her grow hard underneath him, and shuddered at the thought.

"I..." Jack's mouth hovered above Samus's ear. "I want you. Inside me."

"Yeah?"

"Yeah. If you're good..."

"I am. Definitely." Samus laughed as she ran her palms up and down Jack's thighs. "I just have to get you out of my pants."

Jack didn't have to be told twice. They shuffled around on the bed, removing clothing in a matter of seconds. As their mouths met again, Jack could already feel the difference between them. Now, he wasn't as afraid. Samus knew everything. And the suit looked just as good on the bedroom floor as it did on his body. He was sure of that.

"You ready?" Samus asked, trailing kisses along his neck.

"Oh yeah," Jack said. "I'm good."

~~*

In the morning, Jack woke up first. He grabbed his T-shirt from the floor and pulled it over his sports bra. He took his phone as he left the bedroom so he could catch up on messages while Samus continued to sleep. There were several texts from Alicia, most of which involved generic terminology questions, and links to YouTube videos. Most were of popular FTM vloggers, including one singer named Skylar who Jack had watched for hours beforehand.

But before he could get sucked into the vortex of YouTube, Jack pulled up a new email for his mother. He spent at least forty minutes writing it, then fifteen minutes rereading it, before hitting send.

"Good morning." Samus appeared by her kitchen doorway, wearing only her T-shirt and underwear. "You been up long?"

"No." Jack glanced at the oven clock and bit his lip. "Well, maybe a little. I've just been catching up, you know."

"Uh-huh. You email your mom?"

When Jack nodded, Samus walked over to squeeze him in a tight hug. "Good. I'm proud of you. Things will be okay. I know they will."

"And if not?"

"Don't think about that future. Think about a different one. Like me making you breakfast, and us going back to bed." Samus rubbed her hands up and down Jack's back. "Or, if you want to stay awake, we could get a cat. You know? A future like that is worth thinking about."

"It is. You really want that cat, huh?"

"I do! If I get it, would you help name it?"

"Sure. But breakfast first."

"Of course."

Jack smiled. He had a feeling that Samus was right. Over eggs and toast, Jack's phone buzzed again.

"You want me to read it first?" Samus offered. "I think that ring-tone is your mom, right?"

"It is..." Jack sighed. He wanted to do this himself. Don't think about the bad future. Think about the one you want, the one you need. He swiped the lock screen away and opened the message from his mother. After reading the message once, then doubling back to be sure it was for real, all Jack could do was laugh.

Okay, this is interesting. I'll have a lot of questions next time I see you, his mother responded. *But if you don't want to make a dress out of the fabric, will you make me one? Please?*

"I take it that's good news?" Samus asked.

"Oh yeah," Jack said. "Don't worry. Everything's fine."

Epilogue

"Get in close. Closer now. Come on, pretend you love each other."

"Very funny," Jack said. He slid his arm around Samus's waist, inching into her personal space for the photo. Alicia was behind the camera, her hair dyed a bright shade of violet-black to match her purple mini-skirt made with the leftover bits of fabric from the dress Jack had made his mother. He also made Samus a feminine suit jacket out of the same material and a tie for himself.

Delia stood to the side of the display with her own camera. After posing with Samus for Alicia's picture, Jack turned to the left slightly so his mother could also capture them.

"And you too, Alicia," Delia said. "Get in the shot."

Alicia slotted herself on Jack's other side, making him the centre of the picture.

"Beautiful. Thank you." Delia flipped her camera around, admiring the shots she just took. Under the bright spring sunlight, the purple stood out on all their outfits and made them look ridiculously coordinated.

"See?" Delia commented. "I knew that colour was good. I'm so glad it works for you, Samus."

"Me too! Your son is so talented with sewing."

Though Jack's mom sometimes flinched under the male pronouns and titles for Jack, she was coming around. The first week after coming out, there had been a lot of late night talks with both Alicia and Samus to explain all the terms. Sometimes she still messed up, but it was out of habit and not malicious intent. And with time, she'd get a lot better.

Thankfully, and probably the most important thing to Jack at the time, was that Delia was totally okay with him wearing a suit. Jack worked hard the weeks leading up to the convocation ceremony to get the measurements precisely right and it had paid off. Samus's old suit now fit him perfectly. Alicia had given him a shorter and more masculine hair cut and his binder came the day before the ceremony. The school responded to Jack's official change of name form for his diploma, allowing him to receive his degree in Math from Waterloo University under the new name of Jackson Howard Vasquez.

For Jack, it still seemed like a dream. But the more he did, the easier it got. With Samus by his side, he was sure it would keep getting easier.

"Hey, Jack," Alicia called. "You think we should use some of these photos as promos for our business? I mean, you did make half the outfits."

"Yeah! That's a really good idea. You okay with being a model, then, Samus?"

Samus baulked a little at the thought. "Really?"

"Yeah. Why not? You looked really good here." Alicia turned her camera so Samus could see the photos she had already taken. "What do you say? I really dig these two. You guys look sweet."

Samus studied the camera for a moment then nodded. "Okay, sure. Who thought I'd ever be a model, right?"

"I think stranger things have happened," Alicia said, "but that's just me."

"Yeah, like me being in a straight relationship?" Jack suggested with a smirk. As he slid an arm around Samus, she let out a low giggle.

"I do have to admit," Alicia said, flicking and finding the photo she had just taken of the two of them together. "You two really are a model couple. A picture of heterosexuality."

"Oh, what a fantasy!" Samus snickered again.

"Okay, enough bad jokes," Delia stated over the dull roar of the crowd. "Before the ceremony starts and I lose all of you in the crowd, can I have one more photo of just Jack? This is his day, after all."

"It is. I think that's a good idea." Samus squeezed Jack's hand then moved to the sidelines where Alicia was. Jack felt naked without two of his biggest supporters next to him and under the prying eye of his mother. Jack just wanted to be done with school. As much as he liked the pageantry between himself and Samus, it was all a joke, right?

"I'm very proud of you," his mother said between the camera clicks. "Really. I am."

Her voice was genuine. Jack knew it for sure. It was still a little strange to hear, but Jack nodded. "Thank you. I really appreciate it."

"Change your thoughts, change your light," his

mother murmured. "Now smile. Last picture, okay?"

Jack smiled. His mother's words no longer reviled him in the same way they used to. Maybe it was hard for her to understand at first, but whatever New Age-y stuff his mother had been listening to had helped her to understand Jack's transformation or new way of life. *Change your thoughts, change your life,* Jack repeated in his head. As he glanced around at the field filled with people who were about to get their degrees like him, and his supporters in Alicia and Samus, he supposed those simple words were really quite true. *Change your thoughts, change your future.*

When his mother's cell phone rang, she apologized. "It's Jim. He probably needs directions. I'll be behind you soon enough, okay, dear?"

"Sure. No worries. We still have some time."

People were already filtering inside the auditorium. So many years of his life were spent in this school and behind its walls. He was more than ready to break out and leave, without a second thought.

"How are you doing?" Samus asked, sliding a hand around Jack's shoulders. "You going to be okay?"

"Definitely." He squeezed her hand. "You ready?"

"Yeah. I'm just hoping we finish soon, because you know how much Stoker hates it when we leave her alone for too long."

Jack laughed then nodded. "Then we better hurry."

"Wait for me!" Alicia called after them both. Both paused until Alicia was by Jack's side.

"Now are we ready?" Jack asked.

Everyone nodded. Without another word, the three of them stepped inside.

Fin

About the Author

Eve Francis is an f/f romance and erotica author who has appeared in Infernal Ink, In My Bed Magazine, For The Girls, Hot Chili Erotica, Skin to Skin, and Gay Flash Fiction. Eve lives in Canada where they often sleep late, spend too much time online, and repeatedly watch B-horror movies (especially Canadian B-horror movies or those involving inclement weather and sharks). When not writing romances, Eve sometimes dabbles in poetry and speculative fiction, often with romantic overtones. Eve also attends a Canadian university for their PhD, focusing in transgender literature, American fiction, and film adaptation. Basically, Eve gets to spend a lot of time online, read a bunch of awesome trans books, and watch a bunch of cool movies while also teaching some first years how to write an essay. Sweet, right? You should talk to them about transgender issues, LGBT poetry, or cool places to find veggie food in downtown Toronto.

For news and updates about writing, mixed with some random fandom stuff, follow one (or both!) of these:

Website: https://evefrancis.wordpress.com/
Tumblr: paintitback.tumblr.com

Made in the USA
Middletown, DE
20 April 2017